Henry F. Fotheringham

Erskine of Linlathen

Selections and Biography

Henry F. Fotheringham

Erskine of Linlathen
Selections and Biography

ISBN/EAN: 9783743316737

Manufactured in Europe, USA, Canada, Australia, Japa

Cover: Foto ©Raphael Reischuk / pixelio.de

Manufactured and distributed by brebook publishing software
(www.brebook.com)

Henry F. Fotheringham

Erskine of Linlathen

ERSKINE

OF LINLATHEN

Selections and Biography

HENRY F. HENDERSON, M.A.
DUNDEE

OLIPHANT ANDERSON & FERRIER
1899

PRINTED BY

MORRISON AND GIBB LIMITED, EDINBURGH

FOR

OLIPHANT ANDERSON & FERRIER

EDINBURGH AND LONDON

CONTENTS

SELECTIONS

INTRODUCTORY

THE name of Erskine is an honoured one in the annals of Scottish History. Lord Erskine, the brilliant forensic orator, and his brother Harry, the kindly, witty advocate; John of Carnock, the Blackstone of Scottish Jurisprudence; Ebenezer and Ralph Erskine, the noble founders of the Secession, and Thomas Erskine of Linlathen, have made the name illustrious. The last, the subject of this sketch, is perhaps a less familiar name in Scotland than the others, but none of them better deserves to be known than he, both as a man and a leader of religious thought.

His life stretched from 1788 to 1870, and in the course of that long and eventful period he exercised a great influence both at home and in America. The progress and increasing prominence of religious thought that this century has witnessed, the liberation of the mind from hard, unhappy views of Divine truth, the widening and enrichment of the idea of God and of the redemptive purpose of God, the awakening of a new interest in Religion, and the reconciliation of the ethical with the doctrinal contents of the gospel have been perhaps more directly due to the teaching and personal character of Thomas Erskine than to any other single source of influence that can be named. The influence of Robertson of Brighton, which has received a fuller acknowledgment from the Christian Church, comes nearest to that of Erskine; but as a thinker, as well as a personal force, Erskine was of larger account, while as a product of the stiff Calvinistic soil of Scotland, he was a more extraordinary phenomenon.

Those who knew him personally, like the late Bishop Ewing, have dwelt on the difficulty of writing his life. The difficulty arises from the fact that what the biographer has "to depict is spirit and not matter, that he has to convey light, to represent sound, an almost insuperable difficulty." But though the difficulty is not lessened but increased for one who can only claim to be an admiring student of Erskine, surely an attempt may be made to set forth some of the messages that he brought to the world, to estimate the place he occupies in the evolution of religion, and to supply those to whom he is not more than a name with some idea of the exalted goodness of the man.

The author begs to acknowledge the kindness of Professor Knight, LL.D., St. Andrews; Professor T. M. Lindsay, D.D., Glasgow; and David Erskine, Esq., of Linlathen, in reading the proof-sheets and supplying many valuable suggestions. He is specially grateful to Mr. Erskine for permission to photograph the portrait of his distinguished grand-uncle. The photograph, specially taken for this work by Valentine of Dundee, represents Erskine as he appeared in his fifty-ninth year, and is from a portrait in Linlathen House, by John Partridge, portrait painter extraordinary to Her Majesty the Queen and the late Prince Consort.

ERSKINE OF LINLATHEN

HIS ANCESTRY

THOMAS ERSKINE was proud of his ancestry, and had good reason to be proud of it, for, as Principal Shairp said, "on either side he was sprung from a far-descended and gracious race." His great-grandfather was Colonel John Erskine of Carnock, who was the great-great-grandson of the Regent Mar, King James the Sixth's trusty counsellor. The "black colonel," as he was called (on account of his swarthy countenance), was one of the most notable and picturesque figures in Scotland in the eighteenth century.

Ramsay of Ochtertyre, who knew much about him, is perhaps a little hard on the black colonel,

I

although he is not likely very wide of the mark in describing him as "rather a man of the seventeenth than of the eighteenth century; for in church matters he had all the crotchets of the Covenanters, which he inherited from his mother. Although a zealous Whig, he was all his life an irreconcilable enemy to the Union, even after some of its good effects became apparent; but a zealous party man is never to be convinced."[1] A story connected with one of his Covenanter "crotchets" is worth telling. He had been one of those who went to the Hague to bring the Prince of Orange over to England. For this service he was entitled to recognition from his sovereign, and would have received it—as so many of his brother officers did—but for one of his Covenanter "crotchets." In a list which the King had ordered of those entitled to honour, the name of the black colonel was conspicuous by its absence. The explanation was at once given by the Ministers who had prepared the list. The name had been omitted, owing to the black colonel conscientiously refusing to take the oaths of allegiance and abjuration, on the ground that "he would thereby be held as approving of the Constitution of the Church of England and the manner of its connection with the State." When

[1] *Scotland and Scotsmen*, i. 144.

King William heard the explanation, he answered, " It may be so, but I know Lieutenant-Colonel Erskine to be a firmer friend to the Government than many of those who have taken that oath."

This true-blue Presbyterian ancestor of Thomas Erskine's served his King, his Country, and his Church with great-hearted patriotism for more than half a century. He sat both in the Scots and the Imperial Parliaments, and represented the Presbytery of Dunfermline in the supreme Court of the Church for forty years. To a man of his iron constitution these honours probably more than compensated for others he had sacrificed. He was addicted to strange habits. One of them was a passion for litigation, about which Thomas Erskine was fond of relating the following bit of pleasantry. The black colonel's son was John Erskine of Carnock, author of the *Institutes*, who was a quiet peaceably-disposed man, quite unlike his father. When the old man was dying, his litigious habits were sore to part with; at least he is credited with saying, " Haena I thretty gude ga'in pleas on hand, and that fule Jock will hae compounded them a' a fortnicht after I'm dead ! " He seems to have had all the social kind-hearted geniality of the Scottish gentlemen of the eighteenth century, and was fiery tempered withal. A ludicrous instance of his kindly though

peppery temper is still worth relating. It happened at Culross, where he had a house and was
at the time staying, and where on the occasion in
question he had as a visitor his grandson John,
afterwards the celebrated leader of the General
Assembly, then a lad of about fourteen years of age.
On the morning in question the black colonel's
asthma was worse than usual, and he thought that
the fumes of kelp - burning at the shore were
intensifying his distress. Accordingly, he sent
down orders to the river to stop the nuisance; but
his orders were not heeded. Not knowing that
the burning of kelp was carried out with the
sanction of the magistrates of the royal burgh,—
or, to be more correct, utterly disregarding the
authority of these worthy gentlemen,—the colonel
in a rage mounted his horse, drew his sword, and
making his grandson bear it, the two hastened
down to the place of offence. In a small community every action of such a man as the colonel
is closely watched. The circumstance became
known, so that the worthy magistrates—jealous
of their dignity—followed the old man and boy
to the beach, surrounded them, and took them
prisoners. The old colonel immediately came to
his senses, and laughing at the humour of the
situation, exclaimed : " Gentlemen, this is all
nonsense ! We are all in the wrong; come along

to the inn, and let us dine, and forget this folly."

Thomas Erskine's grandfather was John Erskine of Carnock, Professor of Scots Law at Edinburgh, the Blackstone of Scotland, and author of the *Institutes*. Ramsay of Ochtertyre, one of his bosom friends, drew John Erskine's portrait, we may depend upon it, true to the life. His quiet and thoughtful habit of reserve descended to Thomas Erskine. "John Erskine of Carnock," says Ramsay, "deserves honourable mention among the law worthies of those times, though he was nowise ambitious of the palm of eloquence or of celebrity. Of him too I can speak with full confidence, for I was well acquainted with him in his latter years. Indeed, many happy days have I spent either under his roof or that of those who were dearest to him. . . . His excessive diffidence and dislike to disputation, joined to the weakness of his constitution and the extreme feebleness of his voice, forbade all public speaking or anything that required much exertion. But it did not hinder him from studying to excellent purpose; and being esteemed a learned, deserving man, he was made Professor of Municipal Law at Edinburgh, an office which suited his views. In that chair he sat for a number of years, and had the merit of having brought his class into high repute. He contrived to reduce

all he had read upon the law of Scotland, and all
the innovations that had taken place since the
great authors had written, into a regular system,
to the great ease and edification of the students,
whom it saved a great deal of thought and labour.
. . . The preparing this work for the press was
his chief amusement and occupation, after resign-
ing his class and returning to the country. Nor
did he desist from his task when almost worn to
a shadow and his dissolution appeared to be at
no great distance. While sitting at table, or
playing at cards, at which he was very keen, he
would get up and retire to his study to set down
some fact or reflection that struck him at the
moment. Though nearly finished, it was not
published till after his death, when it lost nothing
by being committed to his son David. . . . In
his children he was particularly lucky—the high
character which some of them bore in their professions helping to cast a lustre on his evening of
life. The care and tendance of his family served
indeed as a stay and cordial to his declining years,
which neither wealth nor power could command.
Sir Thomas Browne says that *his* life had been
a miracle of thirty years. With much more propriety might that observation have been applied
to Mr. Erskine, who was for more than forty years
thought to be in a consumption, from spitting

blood, yet lived to the age of seventy with all his faculties entire. After many unexpected escapes from death, this good man at length expired in that happy frame of mind which piety and the remembrance of a well-spent life inspire, in the month of March 1768."[1]

The famous leader of the Evangelicals in the General Assembly, Dr. John Erskine, colleague in Greyfriars of Principal Robertson, was a son of John Erskine, and uncle to Erskine of Linlathen. He too, like his father and grandfather before him, was notable in his time. It was he who in the notorious Assembly of 1796 indignantly prefaced his reply to those who refused to support the cause of Foreign Missions with the memorable words, " Moderator, rax me that Bible." Dr. John Erskine was a remarkable man, and far in advance of his age. The friend of Jonathan Edwards and of Cotton Mather, he set himself at the ripe age of sixty to acquire a knowledge of the Dutch and German languages, in order that he might be able to study continental theology at first hand. All parties and shades of opinion respected him. He combined in an unusual degree the qualities of " rank, piety, and learning." With all his warm religious fervour he had, as his nephew of Linlathen after him also had in pre-eminent degree, a measure

<hr>

[1] *Scotland and Scotsmen*, i. 144.

of magnanimity and tolerance by no means always
characteristic of the party of zeal.   In the case of
Dr. Erskine this fine trait of character was nobly
illustrated on the occasion of his colleague, Principal
Robertson's, death.   The two men, although differing
sharply on all public questions, lived and laboured
amicably together for the long period of twenty
years.   Dr. Erskine's funeral sermon was so sincere
and generous a tribute that Dugald Stewart
remarks in his Life of Robertson, "It would be
difficult to say whether it reflected greater honour
on the character of the writer or of him whom it
commemorates."   The portrait of this interesting
divine in the pulpit, and also out of it, is given in
the pages of *Guy Mannering* with the great wizard's
incomparable art.   Colonel Mannering under the
escort of Lawyer Pleydell resolves to go to church
in Edinburgh to hear the celebrated Robertson,
but it is his distinguished colleague, Erskine, who
mounts the rostrum.

"'And now, sir, if you please, we shall go to the
Greyfriars church, to hear our historian of Scotland, of the Continent, and of America.'

"They were disappointed—he did not preach that
morning.—'Never mind,' said the counsellor, 'have
a moment's patience, and we shall do very well.'

"The colleague of Dr. Robertson ascended the
pulpit.   His external appearance was not pre-

possessing. A remarkably fair complexion, strangely contrasted with a black wig without a grain of powder; a narrow chest and a stooping posture; hands which, placed like props on either side of the pulpit, seemed necessary rather to support the person than to assist the gesticulation of the preacher; no gown, not even that of Geneva, a tumbled band, and a gesture which seemed scarce voluntary,—were the first circumstances which struck a stranger. 'The preacher seems a very ungainly person,' whispered Mannering to his new friend.

"'Never fear, he's the son of an excellent Scottish lawyer—he'll show blood, I'll warrant him.'

"The learned counsellor predicted truly. A lecture was delivered, fraught with new, striking, and entertaining views of Scripture history—a sermon in which the Calvinism of the Kirk of Scotland was ably supported, yet made the basis of a sound system of practical morals, which should neither shelter the sinner under the cloak of speculative faith or of peculiarity of opinion, nor leave him loose to the waves of unbelief and schism. Something there was of an antiquated turn of argument and metaphor, but it only served to give zest and peculiarity to the style of elocution. The sermon was not read—a scrap of paper containing the heads of the discourse was occasionally referred to, and the enunciation, which at first seemed imperfect and embarrassed, became, as the preacher warmed in his progress, animated and distinct; and although the discourse could not be quoted as a correct specimen of pulpit eloquence, yet Mannering had seldom heard so much learning, metaphysical acuteness, and energy of argument, brought into the service of Christianity.

"'Such,' he said, going out of the church, 'must have been the preachers, to whose unfearing minds, and acute, though sometimes rudely exercised talents, we owe the Reformation.'

"'And yet that reverend gentleman,' said Pleydell, 'whom I love for his father's sake and his own, has nothing of the sour or pharisaical pride which has been imputed to some of the early fathers of the Calvinistic Kirk of Scotland. His colleague and he differ, and head different parties in the kirk, about particular points of church discipline; but without losing personal regard or respect for each other, or suffering malignity to interfere in an opposition, steady, constant, and apparently conscientious on both sides.'"[1]

Thomas Erskine's father was David Erskine, W.S., second son of John Erskine of Carnock, by his second marriage. The little we know of him

[1] *Guy Mannering*, ch. xxxvii.

is all to his credit. He died in his prime in 1791 at Naples, whither he had gone in search of health. He had a most successful Edinburgh practice, and was able to purchase Linlathen, an estate in Forfarshire. He was "allowed by all competent judges to have been one of the ablest and most honourable men whom his profession has produced." Thomas, thirty-six years after his father's death, visited Naples, and in the house where his father died wrote the following lines :—

"I have often wished that I had the slightest trace of him in my memory, but I was just two years old when he left home. I know nothing of my father's mind, except very general traits. I don't know how he felt when he knew that he was on the borders of the invisible world. There is something very striking in the relation between a father and a child when death prevents any personal acquaintance between them. When he parted from me he knew as little of me as I did of him, and yet no doubt he felt an interest in me ; but when he looked at me he could no more conjecture what was within me, or what my destiny might probably be, than he could conjecture what was going on in the moon. What a strange interest that is which we can thus take in beings that we are absolutely ignorant of ! I feel a love for my father and a deep interest in him. Are these

earthly connections to extend beyond this world in
any shape ? . . ."[1]

Erskine's mother was one of the Grahams of
Airth.   His grandmother, Mrs. Graham of Airth,
gives his childhood a quaint setting.   She was one
of Prince Charlie's sworn friends, and a rigid
devotee of "black Prelacy."   She held an
Episcopalian service in her house, and refused to
pray for King George.   On Sundays, instead of
attending the parish church, she held this service
iu the castle of Arith at the hour of the public
service.   It was here amid the happiest surround-
ings that much of Erskine's childhood was spent.

In this "ideal abode of an ancient Scottish
family," in the romantic neighbourhood of Falkirk
Muir, the scene of two battles, with the old-
fashioned gardens of Airth to feast in, and the old
oak trees to swing under, how happy the boy must
have been, and what food for his imagination he
must have received.   Erskine had a host of well-
born, highly-endowed kinsmen and kinswomen,
cousins by the score at the family seats of Kippen-
ross, Cardross, and elsewhere, whose friendships
were   tenderer   and   more   intimate   than   blood
relationships often are, and that worked like a spell
upon him in after years.   Erskine never married,
but   no   man   respected   and   appreciated   family

[1] *Letters*, 32.

ties more. He was proud of his blood, of his worthy ancestry, of the honoured name he bore. " I feel an increasing value for those loves and friendships, which I never earned myself, but which were given to me in my birth." The memory of his uncles and aunts was sweeter to him, he confessed, than all the genius of Raphael. On the death of one of them he would weep the whole day. His mother, who died in 1836, received a noble tribute from him. " She has been to us in her relation of mother a most instructive type and witness of the love of God." Of his brother James, who died in early manhood, and whose character left the deepest impression on him, he thus wrote at the time of Madame de Broglie's death : " I always thought James most beautiful, and I thought her most beautiful. They were both like what I can suppose glorified humanity will be." He always encouraged others to be loyal to blood relationship. A fine instance of this was given in his refusal to accept the gift of Jean Paul Richter's portrait from the daughter of that great literary genius. He had made the acquaintance of the lady on one of his visits to the Continent, and with the charm that he had for all good men and women, had so delighted her that she desired him to accept a present of the family relic. But Erskine sent the following reply : " Will you ask Miss Wagner, with my best regards, to let Madame Foster (Richter's daughter) know that I appreciate most highly the kindness of her intention of sending me her father's portrait, but that I entirely coincide with her husband's opinion that it ought not to go out of the family. In fact, though I should have rejoiced to have received it as an expression of love, yet I should also have rejoiced to have sent it back as an act of justice."

ERSKINE'S TEACHERS

Edinburgh High School—Dr. Adam—"Willie brewed a Peck
o' Maut"—Self-improvement—New Species of Country
Gentleman—Influence and Friendship of Dr. Chalmers
—At Paris together—Amusing Blunder there—Thomas
Carlyle, Vinet, William Law.

THOMAS ERSKINE received the best part of his
school training in the High School of Edinburgh,
under the famous Dr. Adam, who had all the
great men of the day through his hands—Scott,
Brougham, Jeffrey, and the rest. Arrayed in the
picturesque habiliments of the eighteenth century—
silk stockings, shoe-buckles, etc.—and carrying the
self-conscious air of the first scholar in Europe,
Adam was a man of great personality and force,
and commanded an extraordinary influence over the
rising generation of Scottish youth, not only by his
fabulous stores of Latinity, but by the excellent
example he set them of industry and hard work.
He spent his life for the school, and in his death-
struggles raved about it. His last words have
never been forgotten: "But it grows dark; boys,
you may go."

Another of Erskine's teachers at the High School was William Nicol, the friend and comrade of Burns, whom the poet has immortalised in the verse :

> "O Willie brew'd a peck o' maut,
>   And Rob and Allan cam to pree :
>   Three blyther hearts, that lee-lang night,
>   Ye wadna found in Christendie."

Nicol was an assistant under Adam, and seems to have been a terror to the school. At Dowie's tavern of an evening—the howff of many of the literati—Nicol grew balmy and genial, but in the daytime at school he seems to have been a *gey gruesome carle*, and, according to Lockhart, to have even been "inhumanly cruel to the boys under his charge." In the absence of detailed information concerning Erskine's life at school and college, we can easily imagine the benefits he must have derived from coming in contact with a scholar like Adam and a friend of poets like the irascible Nicol. What was of even greater moment for a lad cradled in ease and comfort, was the rough and tumble existence of the playground, and the healthy mixture of the benches, country gentlemen's sons and city shopkeepers' sitting cheek-by-jowl and competing for the same prizes.

Erskine went next to a Durham school for a short time, preparatory to his returning to Edinburgh

to study for the bar. At seventeen we find him
keeping a diary, a usual procedure among old and
young long ago; but he gave it up, he tells us,
because he " did not do it truly." About the same
time he read one of John Foster's essays, "On a Man
Writing Memoirs of Himself." From the perusal of
that famous work his mind received a bias which it
never afterwards lost; and he imbibed ideas that
were destined to influence him to the last, and
through him many others in the world. Foster's
ideal man goes through life, noting as he goes,
whatever habits and views arise within him; and
tracing them, at the same time, to their proper
sources within himself, and all with the view of
educating and improving character. This idea cap-
tivated young Erskine's mind, and taught him to
regard life in a more serious light than he had formerly done. Life was given for the education of character, and was therefore invested with new grandeur
and with increased responsibility. This increased
responsibility seemed to him " of such a solemn and
overpowering weight, that a continual receiving of
help from on high was essential to our success, and
a continual looking to God for that help was our
first duty and our chief privilege." This was the
period when serious thoughts took possession of
Erskine's mind.

It is nothing derogatory to the honourable pro-

2

fession of law, for which Erskine was destined, to say that a young man—disposed as he was to serious views, and to ruminations on deep religious themes—was not exactly the kind of man to cut a great figure at the bar. Happily for him he was not required very long to pace the weary round of a briefless barrister's existence. By his brother's lamented death, and his succession in consequence to the estate of Linlathen, he was taken from the Parliament House to the more agreeable sphere of a country gentleman's life. Certainly he must have seemed to the lairds of Forfarshire a new species of country gentleman; for however heavy his new duties as laird of Linlathen may have been, and they were considerable, he never permitted them or anything else to interrupt his serious studies, or retard the growth and development of his thoughts.

In 1818 he made the acquaintance of one who was destined to influence him considerably—Dr. Chalmers. Chalmers was then minister of the Tron Kirk, Glasgow, and was electrifying the merchant princes of the West with the famous Astronomical Discourses. The acquaintanceship was started through Erskine's connexion with a country mansion in the neighbourhood of Glasgow. Cadder House had been a kind of second home to him ever since the marriage of his sister Christian to Charles Stir-

ling, a younger son of Keir. There we find him in
later years studying his favourite Plato, recovering
from an attack of influenza, and gaining the quiet and
composure needful for writing his book on Election.
On the occasion of his first visit to Dr. Chalmers,
Chalmers' diary contains the following entry:—
" Mr. Erskine of Linlathen called between one and
two o'clock, and spent the day with me. . . . I
have had a great treat in Mr. Erskine, a holy,
spiritual, enlightened, and affectionate Christian,
who is also a man of great property and of great
literature." Chalmers greatly enjoyed Erskine's
society, and acknowledged that he derived great
spiritual benefit from his visits. Referring to them
in 1823, the warm-hearted divine confessed that
" the impulse of these visits remains, and this day I
have proposed on a more distinct and strenuous work
of sanctification, and shall allow, if God will, much
larger space than before for the employment of
daily and direct communion with Himself." The
benefits of the friendship on the other side were
equally great, and as generously acknowledged.
Erskine learned to trust Chalmers like a father,
and to open out all his mind to him. He sent him
the first draft of his earliest book, and felt at
liberty to ventilate his peculiar views in Chalmers'
presence. How much he owed to Dr. Chalmers
may be gathered from the following fine tribute, to

be found in the first of his published letters :—" You have been very much followed by great and small, by learned and ignorant, and yet you listened with the meek candour of a learner to one whom you could not but consider as your inferior by far. If you had opened to me all mysteries and all knowledge, you could not have brought to my conscience the strong conviction of the necessity and the reality of Christianity with half the force that this deportment of yours impressed upon me.

" I need not say how delighted I should be were you to favour me with a visit to Linlathen. I never expect an answer to my letters from you, so anything in that way will be only an unlooked-for pleasure, as I know the scantiness of your time."

Erskine was Dr. Chalmers' fellow-traveller and cicerone in Paris and elsewhere in 1838. Erskine said that on that occasion the activity of Chalmers' intelligence, as well as his benevolence and naïveté, struck everyone whom they met; but he kept silence on a droll accident that befell them in the French capital, which Chalmers reports with great glee in his diary. On entering their Paris lodging one day, Chalmers was informed by the servant that the English Ambassador had called on him in his absence. Should he return the call ? Erskine thought he should, and the two sallied forth in the direction of the great man's house. The great

personage was also out, luckily ; but unluckily Dr.
Chalmers left his card. The rest of the story may
be told in Chalmers' own words: " On returning met
a Dr. Wright, who cleared up the mystery of the
provoking and ludicrous mistake. *He* had called,
given his designation to the porter of *Ministre de
l'Eglise*, understood by him as *le Ministre Anglais*,
and left me in a state of uncertainty whether to
laugh or to cry at the absurdity of the whole transaction."

The friendship did not become closer or more
sympathetic with advancing years, though it remained warm to the end. We find Erskine saying,
" I had a letter from Dr. Chalmers the other day
proving that he had completely misunderstood my
book. I need not think of writing another book to
explain the book which I have already written."
Probably both men failed to understand one another
fully. At least Erskine did not speak much of
Chalmers after 1843, nor did he seem fully to appreciate the great events that were then happening, and
in which Dr. Chalmers took so distinguished a part.
In early days, however, as we have seen, they understood and helped one another. Chalmers even
intrusted Erskine with the task of composing an
introductory essay to an edition of Baxter's *Saint's
Rest*, brought out under his editorship.

There were three Scotsmen of the name of

Thomas, during the second quarter of the century, who influenced one another, and influenced the world—Thomas Chalmers, Thomas Erskine, and Thomas Carlyle. With regard to the influence of Carlyle, although Erskine's principal works had been given to the world before Carlyle appeared in his literary prime, he also was one of the teachers who helped Erskine, and whom he in turn helped. " I love the man . . . he has a real belief in the invisible, which, in these railroad and steam-engine days, is a great matter. He sees and con-demns the evil and baseness of living in the lower part of our nature, instead of living in the higher. He is full of thoughts, of genius, of information." So Erskine wrote in the beginning of 1843. What Erskine valued from the beginning of his life, and increasingly with advancing years, was reality. In fact it may be said that he toiled after it, as others have toiled after fortune. He laboured almost to the pitch of agony, in order to make the invisible world a reality to men, and to turn the dogmatic formulas of tradition into the living language of everyday life. For that reason he loved Carlyle, and recognised in him a brother in arms. The two men differed from one another as day differs from night in mental habits, in personal disposition, in philosophic principles. But they had this in common, that in an age that had its own fair share

of insincerity and sham alike in the religious and
the political world, these twain stood forth for truth,
for reality, for solidity, as against flippancy, super-
ficiality, falsehood. Erskine's chief concern was
for religion, and for truth and reality in religion.
That comes out again and again.

"Dear Friend,—I do not say that the inward
revelation in conscience makes us independent of
the outward revelation, but I say that we never
rightly receive or believe the outward revelation
until we learn it from the inward, and that the
use of the outward is to foster and educate the
inward."

"All that a man learns from the Bible without
its awakening within him a living consciousness of
its truth, might as well not be learned."

A man's worth, according to Erskine, was in the
exact ratio of his reliableness, his veracity. He
wrote to Dean Stanley, for instance, about the
integrity of John Bright, whose speeches he ex-
ceedingly admired. "I wonder whether he is a
man really and sincerely desirous of doing what is
right, and whether the frequent introduction of
such words as humanity and justice and Christianity indicates something real in his heart and
conscience." Frederick Denison Maurice was
Erskine's ideal man, and of him he said: "As
Erasmus described the difference between himself

and Luther, when some flattering friend was giving
him the first place, by saying, I can write, but
Luther can burn, *Maurice can do both.*"

There were other living teachers who profoundly
influenced Erskine, as Edward Irving, A. J. Scott
(Principal of Owens College), Macleod Campbell of
Row, Bishop Ewing, and F. D. Maurice. He
learned much from contact with friends on the
Continent, Vinet pre-eminently, " the Pascal of the.
Reformed Church." In the best religious circles
on the Continent, as at home, in the early years of
the century, the influence of Wesley and the
English revival had brought forth some fruits that
were not altogether so wholesome as might have
been desired. Great good had accompanied the
movement unquestionably—the tide of eighteenth-
century indifference had been stemmed—but many
had come to espouse opinions that were nearly as
bad as infidelity itself, by reason of their harshness
and illiberality. Vinet and other liberal-minded
evangelicals on the Continent set themselves to
avert the catastrophe that was impending. He
and the Lausanne circle strove to reconcile culture
and Christianity. He claimed for unregenerate
human nature that it has in it many noble
elements, many surviving traces of God. Without
departing one step from true evangelical teaching,
and with the view of recovering the ethical ele-

ment that was being lost sight of, Vinet emphasised subjective over objective Christianity. " The gospel is believed," he said, " when it ceases to be external and becomes a fact of our consciousness." Christianity to him was conscience raised to its highest exercise. In such an atmosphere Erskine could not but feel at home. He learned much from Vinet, who, dying early in life, drew from him the well-deserved tribute : " I have always regarded his friendship as one of my most precious possessions, gratifying to my feelings and profitable to my soul, calling me from all low and worldly thoughts to the pursuit of what was imperishable." Such ideas as Vinet and Erskine each in his own way circulated, the importance of conscience as a high court of appeal on all matters pertaining to religion, for instance, were not mere academical questions without importance for the practical governance of life. Far from it. They belonged to the category of forces that in every civilised country have brought about revolutions. Vinet taught that religion to be genuine must be inward, and that conscience was the last criterion of truth, and these ideas made history in his own romantic fatherland, as he and others found to their cost. From what he believed and taught, it followed that no state or hierarchy or ecclesiastical court can be allowed to usurp the authority of conscience ; and

that all attempts to do so must be resisted. It is
our duty to educate the conscience, to liberalise it,
to emancipate it from its prejudices, to plead with
and to persuade it; but to attempt to carry the
citadel by storm is to disown the deepest principles
of Christianity, the religion of inwardness and
conscience. These views ultimately carried Vinet
and his friends out of the State Church of Switzerland, about the same time that similar ideas were
accomplishing similar results in Scotland.

Passing from the influence of living teachers to
that of books, Erskine's writings bear the mark
of William Law more perhaps than that of any
other writer. He came under the influence of
Law at an impressionable period of his life,
through reading two of his books, *The Spirit of
Prayer* and *The Spirit of Love*, which represent the
later and more mystical stage of Law's development.
That remarkable writer had made an impression
both on Wesley and Whitfield, and had drawn
forth commendations from Gibbon, Dr. Samuel
Johnson, and John Sterling, for his qualities as a
controversialist and teacher of practical divinity.
Erskine's opinion of Law was formed in 1827 : " I
have been reading a very curious book lately by
Law, the author of *The Serious Call*; it is entitled
The Spirit of Prayer; most mystical it is, but most
beautiful. It is not the gospel, but I think it

may be profitably read by those who know the gospel. . . .

"I wish you would read *The Spirit of Prayer* and *The Spirit of Love*, two works by Law, the author of *The Serious Call*, and tell me what you think of them. I have been much struck by them. There is a great spirituality in them. I like them very much better than Mr. Irving's *Prophecies*. They are, however, very mystical, and if your taste is much averse to mysticism, you may not like them. But I think that you can scarcely help liking them, such a view they give of the love of our God and of that intimate and blessed and glorious union with Himself to which He hath called us." [1]

Law drew Erskine to the mysticism of St. John and the Neo-Platonists, and to the rejection of all that savoured of harshness and arbitrariness in current theology. According to Law, transubstantiation was an innocent and tolerable error compared to the ordinary representation of Election and Reprobation. True religion was inward, spiritual, reasonable. Christ was in every man. It will show the influence to which Erskine at an early age succumbed if we quote Law's own words from the first of the two works recommended to the attention of friends in the foregoing extracts:

[1] *Letters*, 32, 36.

" Men may divide themselves, to have God to themselves: they may hate and persecute one another for God's sake: but this is a blessed Truth that neither the Hater nor the Hated can be divided from the one, holy, Catholic God who, with an unalterable Meekness, Sweetness, Patience, and Goodwill towards all, waits for all, calls for all, redeems them all, and comprehends all in the outstretched arms of His Catholic Love. Ask not therefore how we shall enter into this Religion of Love and Salvation: for it is itself entered into us; it has taken possession of us from the Beginning. It is *Immanuel* in every human soul: it lies as a Treasure of Heaven and Eternity in us: it cannot be divided from us by the Power of Man: we cannot lose it ourselves: it will never leave us nor forsake us, till with our last Breath we die in the Refusal of it. This is the open Gate of our Redemption: we have not far to go to find it. It is every Man's own Treasure: it is a Root of Heaven, a Seed of God, sown into our Souls by the Word of God: and like a small grain of Mustard-seed has a Power of growing to be a Tree of Life. Here, my Friend, you should, once for all, mark and observe *where* and *what* the true Nature of Religion is: for here it is plainly shown you that its Place is within: its Work and Effect is *within*: its Glory, its Life, its Perfection is all within: it is merely and solely the raising a new Life, new Love, and a new Birth in the inward Spirit of our Hearts." . . .

"Ask now what Hell is ? It is Nature destitute of the Light and Spirit of God, and full only of its own Darkness : nothing else can make it to be Hell. Ask what Heaven is ? It is Nature quickened, enlightened, blessed, and glorified by the Light and Spirit of God dwelling in it. What Possibility therefore can there be of our dividing from Hell or parting with all that is hellish in us but by having the Life, Light, and Spirit of God living and working in us ? "[1]

An impressionable mind might easily have been carried away under Law's influence past the bounds of reason and sober thinking, after the manner of Law himself. But Erskine was not so carried away. He had a mind of his own. We see this in the fact that while he cordially took over some of Law's principles, he as heartily rejected others of them. For instance, he had no sympathy with Law's contempt for Manuals of Devotion, nor did he in the least concern himself with Law's fantastic cosmogony, demonology, anthropology, or other theological extravagances, which are remarkable in a writer of Law's strength and sanity. Erskine was not interested in *the Astral Man, the Malady of Nature, the Abode of the Dragon.* He was too

[1] Law's *Spirit of Prayer* and *Spirit of Love.*

sane and robust for that.   What he was interested
in was how to think of God and divine things,
and he learned from Law to regard religion after
a more spiritual and reasonable manner than was
common in his day.   He learned also how to rescue
religion from the contempt into which it had so
generally fallen, and to breathe into its dry bones
the breath of a new life.

ERSKINE'S BOOKS AND LITERARY WORK

ERSKINE made his first appearance in the theological
field in 1820. In that year he published a defence
of Christianity, which he modestly entitled, *Remarks
on the Internal Evidence for the Truth of the Christian
Religion*. The book created a profound sensation.
In the course of nine years it passed into nine editions,
was translated into French in 1822, and into German three years later. Vinet was attracted by it,
and commended it for its "simplicity, conviction,
ardour, new and interesting points of view." J. H.
Newman also read it, and lifted up his anathema
upon it: "A very peculiar and subtle form of Ra-

tionalism that exists covertly in the popular religion
of the day." He was kind enough, however, to
believe that the author was better than his creed.
In America *The Internal Evidence* created an epoch.
President Porter of Yale communicated this grateful
intelligence to the author : " My father, who has
been pastor of one flock for nearly sixty years, said
that the book had done more than any single book
of his time to give character to the new phase of
theology in New England in which Dr. L. Beecher,
Dr. Moses Stuart, and many others were prominently
concerned. The volume is still esteemed very
highly for its arguments and its just discrimination
between the theology of the schools and the theology
of the Scriptures."

Without entering on a discussion of Erskine's
peculiar ideas, it may be well to say something
here regarding his point of view in this, the
earliest, and, in some ways, the most delightful of
his books. He sets out with the conception that
the aim and programme of Christianity is the moral
one of bringing the character of man into harmony
with the character of God. At least that is its
principal aim and purpose. Now, in order to the
accomplishment of this great end, to bring the
creature into moral harmony with the Creator, it
was necessary that the character of the Creator
should be as fully as possible made known to man,

and that in forms best adapted to the end in view.
Natural religion of itself was unequal to this task,
not because of any defect in the kind of information it supplied, but because it was in the habit of
imparting its ideas in forms so abstract and unreal
as to carry with them very little moral effect.   The
heart cannot be healed by abstract terms and
philosophical theorisings.   It cries out for a living
God.   Jesus Christ therefore came into the world
and announced a message which contained a " moral
dynamic."   Christianity is thus superior to any
religion of the natural conscience.   " It presents a
history of wondrous love, in order to excite gratitude ; of high and holy worth, to attract veneration
and esteem.   It presents a view of danger to produce alarm, of refuge to confer peace and joy, and
of eternal glory to animate hope."

In this as in all his books, Erskine bestows
great attention upon the death of Christ, and, as
was natural to him, regards it from the subjective
and moral point of view rather than from the legal
and objective one.   At the same time, the legal
aspect is not by any means left out of sight.   So
far from this, he firmly repudiates the idea of
reducing the great mystery to the level of a mere
piece of moral mechanism.   " These sufferings are
the foundations of a Christian's hope before God,
not only because he sees in them a most marvellous

3

proof of the divine love, but also because he sees in them the sufferings of the Representative of sinners. He sees the denunciations of the law fulfilled, and the bitter cup of indignation allotted to the apostasy drained to the very dregs, and he thus perceives that God is just even when justifying the guilty."

The *Internal Evidence* is pre-eminently a book for the faithful, to confirm them in their faith, and to that extent it will still be found one of the most valuable contributions to the literature of Christian apologetics in the English language. It is, however, of less importance as a defence of Christianity addressed to sceptics and infidels. It errs by going too far in one direction, and not far enough in another. Christianity, if it is to stand solitary and supreme among religions, must be more than an improved edition of natural theology, must have some other distinctiveness than mere personal accentuation. A system of truth that corresponds evidently to man's primitive instincts needs no transcendental origin. St. Paul argued out the matter on different lines. He emphasised the note of divergence. To him Christianity was a new thing under the sun, a revelation unique and unsearchable, a mystery hidden from the past generations. All the same, Erskine has put into this book something nobler and more inspiring than logic, even a spirit of gentleness and peace, that entitles it to live. Dogmatical and denunciatory as he is in many parts of the book, the author is so seriously intent on the reader's spiritual improvement, so earnest in his desire to rescue religion from the barren wastes of unreality into which it has fallen, that he never once descends from his calm position to the shiftiness of ordinary theological controversy.

The *Internal Evidence* was followed, in 1822, by *An Essay on Faith*, which in like manner attained quite a remarkable circulation. In a few years it passed into five editions, and was published in Paris under the title, *Essai sur La Foi*. This was the period of Erskine's greatest productiveness. In 1828 he published *The Unconditional Freeness of the Gospel*, a work which, like its predecessors, attained a high place among the better class of religious people, both at home and on the Continent. Dr. Chalmers, in his great-hearted manner, gave it cordial welcome, and took it for the *Marrow of Modern Divinity* modernised. He pronounced it one of the most delightful books that had ever been written. But Erskine's liberalism went further than that of the Marrow men, and Chalmers had to qualify his praise. He more than suspected that Erskine's teaching was bound to carry him farther out to sea than he himself knew. " I don't like," said

Chalmers, " narrowing the broad basis of the gospel
to the pin-point speculations of an individual brain.
One thing I fear. I do fear that the train of his
thoughts might ultimately lead Mr. Erskine to
doubt the eternity of future punishments. Now,
that would be going sadly against Scripture."

Erskine's next venture was *The Brazen Serpent,
or Life coming through Death*, which first appeared
in 1831, and in a subsequent edition in 1846. At
the time he wrote *The Brazen Serpent* he was more
than usually conscious of enjoying communion with
God. Probably it was this that made him write
with more confidence than usual, almost in the
"Thus saith the Lord" style of an old Hebrew
prophet. Whatever the readers of his book might
think of the historical treatment of the subject,
whether his views of the history were just or not,
of this he was convinced, that his book contained
much of the meaning of Christianity. His only
prolix work appeared in 1837, and with fitting
prolixity is entitled, *The Doctrine of Election, and its
connexion with the General Theory of Christianity,
illustrated from many parts of Scripture, and especially from the Epistle to the Romans*. We find
here many of Erskine's most striking thoughts on
the subject of Conscience, and with a wonderful
ingenuity he brings the fundamental teaching of
Christianity home to the modern conscience, by

showing that each individual man is a little world in himself in which the tragedies of the Betrayal and Crucifixion are being enacted and reproduced.

With the exception of a book on the gifts of the Holy Spirit, introductory essays to Gambold's works, the *Saints' Rest*, the *Letters of Rutherfurd*, and *Extracts of Letters to a Christian Friend*—all published between 1820 and 1830—Erskine gave nothing more to the press until the posthumous work, *The Spiritual Order and other Papers*, appeared in 1871. In *The Spiritual Order* we find this fine piece of religious autobiography.

"When I ask myself what reason or right I have to believe that the Great Being who made and orders all things really cares for men, and has a purpose of good for them in all the circumstances of their lot, it is not enough to answer that I have read this in a very ancient book, or been taught it by a venerable Church. There are objections to such belief which require a more thorough answer: I must myself see and handle its truth. And when I carry my questioning a little further, and ask myself what reason or right I have to believe that a man who lived in Palestine eighteen hundred and sixty years ago was the Son of God, in order to be certain that in this belief I have hold of a substance and not of a mere shadow, I must discern in the history itself a light and truth which will meet the demands both of my reason and conscience. . . . It has been the chief aim of my life to possess such an apprehension of the truth of Christianity as this, and it is now forty-five years since I ventured to give through the press an utterance to this desire, and to accompany it with a sketch of the meagre progress I had then made in realising it. I was brought up from my childhood in the belief of the supernatural and miraculous in connection with religion, especially in connection with the person and life and teaching of Jesus Christ: and like many in the present day, I came in after-life to have misgivings as to the , credibility of this wonderful history. But the patient study of the narrative and of its place in the history of the world, and the perception of a light in it which entirely satisfied my reason and conscience, finally overcame these misgivings and forced on me the conviction of its truth. A good deal of this cannot perhaps be fully communicated to others, but of that which can I wish to record, as distinctly as I am able, what, having found helpful to myself, I think may perhaps be helpful to them." [1]

It is not a little strange that during the long period extending from 1840 till his death in 1870, Erskine should not have published a single book. It is difficult to account for these years of

[1] *The Spiritual Order*, p. 81.

silence. Up till the time when he ceased writing
he had contrived to employ almost every known
means of communicating his ideas to his fellow-
men. He acted till that time on the conviction
that if one has aught to communicate to his
fellow-men, the communication of it is a debt
which man owes to man. He wrote books,
he addressed meetings, he gathered friends and
neighbours into the servants' hall at Linlathen, he
even occupied the pulpit of a chapel in the
neighbourhood regularly on the Sundays. The
conversation usual in society, " where everything
that is most intimate and inward to the conscience
and the heart is studiously suppressed, and where
consequently all life becomes a dead convention-
ality," Erskine could never tolerate. It would
appear, however, that after 1840 he gave up
instructing men in the mass in all these favourite
ways of his. This is certainly strange, and
different from what we would have expected.
We would have expected more literary activity
rather than less for some years to come, at least
after the time at which it all mysteriously came to
an end. He was not an old man at that time, and
during the years that followed he enjoyed the
stimulus of the best company that ever visited in a
country-house. Linlathen during these years was a
shrine that drew to it the finest spirits of the time.

It may be that his still small voice was hushed to
silence, by reason of the ecclesiastical clamour that
was thundering all around.   At anyrate, from
1844 to 1846 we find him in Rome and his
beloved Florence, safe from the strife of tongues.
It is probable that ill-health explains much, and
especially a certain dissatisfaction and disappointment with the popular mind, leading him to suppose
that his task now lay in guiding and influencing
individual minds, rather than in addressing the
world at large; the more especially as individual
minds of the choicest, most sympathetic, and most
teachable order now began to assemble in his
pleasant home at Linlathen autumn by autumn.

However we attempt to explain the silence
that suddenly overtook this noble spirit, it was a
strange and unlooked-for catastrophe, and one
which thousands of cultured and earnest people
in all lands who had benefited by his teaching
deeply deplored.   There is no reason to suppose
that his interest in his favourite subjects lessened
with advancing years.   On the contrary, his
interest in these subjects, and the conformity of
his beautiful character to the truths he taught,
are said by those who knew him best to have
become more apparent year by year.   But it
is not for us to complain.   Thomas Erskine has
given us much.   The nineteenth century has cer-

tainly not produced many Scotsmen who have
made the same rich contributions to the permanent
religious literature of the Victorian era.   Compared
with other writers of religious books, Erskine had
many advantages.   For one thing, he had abundant
leisure ; above all, he had " a heart at leisure from
itself."   Owing to weak eyesight he was not a man
as widely read as he might have been, but the
authors he had read were of the best, and these he
had mastered.   Homer, Plato, Shakespeare, he read
through continuously.   He read the Old and New
Testaments in their original tongues.   While he was
a lad, as we have seen, he seems to have come under
the influence of John Foster's *Essays*, and must have
been powerfully stirred by the trenchant castigation
that current evangelicalism receives at Foster's
hands.   Foster complains that men of taste are
needlessly averted from religion by the poor style
and literary blemishes of writers of religious books.
On young Erskine, Foster's criticisms doubtless had
the effect of making him say, Let me avoid these
faults : let me write in the best manner possible.
Why should the devil have all the good music,
why turn men of taste from Christianity by bad
grammar and coarse similes ?   It is on record that
the Anti-Burgher Synod had cautioned " those who
may be pointing towards public work in the
Church against an affected pedantry of style and

pronunciation *and politeness of expression,*[1] and
James Thomson, who had aspired to the ministry,
had had his exegetical exercise and addition
rejected owing to an "offensive" profusion of fine
writing! The Moderates, indeed, prided themselves
on the excellence of their literary style. Jupiter
Carlyle had said, "I must confess that I do not
love to hear this Church called a poor Church, or
the poorest Church in Christendom. . . . I dislike
the language of whining and complaint. We are
rich in the best goods a Church can have—the
learning, the manners, and the character of its
members. There are few branches of literature in
which the ministers of this Church have not excelled. There are few subjects of fine writing in
which they do not stand foremost in the ranks of
authors, which is a prouder boast than all the pomp
of the hierarchy. . . . Who have written the best
histories, ancient and modern?—It has been clergy-
men of the Church of Scotland. Who has written
the clearest delineation of the human understanding and all its powers?—A clergyman of this
Church. Who has written the best system of
rhetoric, and exemplified it by his own writing?—A
clergyman of this Church. Who wrote a tragedy
that has been deemed perfect?—A clergyman of
this Church. Who was the most perfect mathe-

[1] *Scotland and Scotsmen,* ii. 29.

matician of the age in which he lived?—A clergyman of this Church. Let us not complain of
poverty. It is a splendid poverty indeed. It is
paupertas fecunda virorum." [1]

If we overlook the pomposity of the passage,
it will now be agreed that the Prince of Moderates
was justified in boasting of such "splendid poverty."
But the party who subscribed themselves evangelical
at that time could not see anything to glory in.
They abhorred Moderatism and all its works,
rhetoric and *belles - lettres* included. And so it
came to pass that at the time when Thomas
Erskine began to think for himself, and to blow
upon the dry bones of Scottish theology the breath
of a gracious and reasonable evangelicalism, he
immediately arrested the thoughtful classes of his
time not only by the freshness of his ideas, but by
the chaste beauty and elevation of his language.
It was delightful to Scottish ears to hear one of
themselves discourse on the " Love of God " and the
" Mission of the Incarnate Word " and on the duty
of " Hearing the voice of the Spirit," and handle
these important but at the time discredited themes,
not only with great earnestness and enlightenment,
but with a taste and a felicity of language that
was worthy of Addison or Steele.

Many of the matters on which Erskine wrote

[1] *Autobiography of Dr. Carlyle of Inveresk*, p. 561.

had been for long in Scotland subjects of heated controversy, and had been written about in angry unchristian manner—in the "*thou vain heretic and runagate*" temper—as though errors of the understanding were among the blackest crimes. Erskine introduced a new spirit into the controversial arena, and wrote, mindful of his own and his opponent's liability to err, after the manner of John Knox when he composed his Confession of Faith, and of Cromwell when he besought the Assembly in the bowels of Christ to believe that they might be mistaken. Erskine has left a fine example behind him to theologians and to religious controversialists. He never wavers in his views as if disposed to be shifty, and he can lay about him with his weapons in a manner that leaves nothing to be desired. But he keeps his temper, and tears an opinion to shreds without rending in pieces the life of the unfortunate holder thereof. Besides, there was in him a rich vein of poetry, that gave colour to the subject, and relieved it of the grey gloom in which it had been usually so thickly enveloped. He had strong imaginative power, and could see a great deal that escapes the eye of the mere exegete and grammarian. It was not only that he put vivid colouring and music into his words. His imagination was a visual faculty, by which he was enabled to see in the world of

spirit more than catches the eye of the ordinary
man ; and to trace, and even discover, the working
of laws that the ordinary man altogether passes by.
He could draw pictures with a free and firm hand :
and did this with such masterliness and truth that
metaphor, simile, or historical illustration served the
twofold purpose of illumination and demonstration.
Thus in speaking of what he knew so well, the uses
and meaning of life's trials, he compares them to
the private cypher agreed upon between the Saviour
and the saved ; at another time he calls them the
gymnastics of the heart : " It is no difficulty to me
that so many people are placed in circumstances for
which they are not fitted.   I have felt all my life
that I was in circumstances for which I was not
fitted, and I see that this is necessary.   Education
would stop if we and our circumstances fitted each
other.   Failure is no difficulty to me, or rather there
can be no failure ; for the purpose of God is the
training of the spirit, and this cannot fail.   All
that we are accustomed to value, all that we make
an object of, is just mere gymnastics.   It is
nothing if it does not help forward this."

Erskine, like a true poet, used metaphors not
as mere ornaments to deck out language, but as
illustrations of the things he had seen with the
inner eye.   Calvin, as we might expect, was sparing
in his use of illustrations, but a striking one occurs

somewhere in the *Institutes*. He compares the Bible
to a pair of spectacles, by the use of which we get
a clearer vision of God. Erskine turned that idea
to better account. What the magnifying glass is to
the eye, that, he declared, the Bible is to conscience :
" As the telescope does not change the faculty of
sight, but brings more objects within its range, so
does the Bible to the conscience." Again, one of
his most interesting " finds " in the field of analogy
is used to bring out the true relation of dogma
and duty. " There seems to me," he says, " to
lurk the idea that the dogmas of Christianity are
imposed on us not as helps or guides, but as exercises of obedience and submission. I believe, on
the contrary, that they are given for the purpose of
explaining to us our relations with the spiritual
world. What are the dogmas suited to domestic
life ? Suppose a man entering as a stranger into
a house from which he had been carried away as
an infant, and needing guidance for his conduct
there. The dogmas would be, ' that old man is
your father, that old woman your mother ; these are
uncles and aunts, brothers and sisters ; there is an
old servant who saved your life in your childhood,'
etc. etc. We don't know our duties apart from our
relations, and the knowledge of our relations helps
us to the performance as well as the knowledge of
our duties. To suppose that such domestic truths

are, in the case supposed, given as exercises of faith,
and to be received whether understood or not, would
be too absurd; and yet it would be less absurd than
in the case of the Christian dogmas, because these
are not merely facts, but the vehicles and expressions of principles recognisable by our spiritual
understanding as eternal and necessary truths.
Plato's doctrine of ἀνάμνησις would be a help
to them if they would use it." [1]

Again, for an example of visual imagination,
take that well-sustained parable of St. John and
Barabbas.

" If you could suppose the spirit of a loving man
like St. John imprisoned in the breast of a violent
murderer like Barabbas, you could not doubt but
that he would feel himself agonised and jarred
every moment by the contact of the selfish cruelty
with which he was environed.   And yet his
suffering would not arise simply or chiefly from
the discrepancy between himself and Barabbas, but
because he would feel that Barabbas was still his
fellow-creature, his brother, and he would not be
able to endure the thought that his brother should
be under the influence of this fearful spiritual
malady.   In fine, it would not be disapprobation
merely, but love, that would produce his suffering.
And thus, though free leave were given to him to

[1] *Letters*, 203.

go out from that prison-house, he would say, ' I
cannot go; I must remain till I bring back this
poor brother out of hatred into love, out of self
into God.' And thus would he continue in him,
suffering for him, the just for the unjust, that he
might bring him back to God. And when Barabbas
melted under this suffering love, when he also
began to suffer in the thought of having outraged
duty and outraged love, when he became partaker
of John's sufferings, he would be brought back to
God. What I have supposed John to do in the
case of Barabbas, I believe in truth and in fact to
be done by Jesus Christ in the case of every human
being. I believe that He is in every man, and
that it is His suffering voice which speaks in the
conscience of every man. I believe that He is
thus suffering for every man, the just for the
unjust, that He may bring us back to God. I
believe thus that the recorded history of our Lord
in the Gospels is the outward and objective manifestation of a great subjective truth which is
going on, and which will go on until every soul of
man is brought back to God. And I am sure that
the sorrow which holy love feels for sin is the true
essential and divine medicine for sin. I believe
that the knowledge of the distinction between
right and wrong is a most precious gift, and yet
I believe that it cannot alone accomplish the

task of turning man's heart from self to God. We need to know that the voice which in conscience speaks to us of right and wrong is the voice of a love which suffers when we do wrong, and must continue to suffer until we return from self to God." [1]

It is interesting to see that the hypothesis of natural law in the spiritual world was present to Erskine's mind more than thirty years ago, though he had the sobriety not to press it too far. "Christianity itself," he says, "has more analogy with natural science than with history. It is a revelation of laws that are independent of facts. There must be a centre of gravity in the moral world which when once found we shall be right, like the planets, not only as to that centre, but to everything else." "The planets move in orderly circles because they have a right centre ;—we have disorderly motions because we have a wrong centre. The way to get right is to get into the right place, not to go on trying very hard to be right where we are."

One can form an idea of Erskine's power of elevated expression in the following extract from a letter to Miss Julia Wedgwood. As an example of what Nature yields up to the man of devout feeling and kindly eye, it is worthy of

[1] *Letters*, 164.

4

Wordsworth.   Erskine was in his eightieth year at the time.

"In my drives I generally go out towards the west, and, of course, return with my face towards the east.   During the winter I was attracted and interested by the frequent recurrence of the same natural phenomenon.   The moon rose a little before the sun set, and had just the appearance of a thin bit of fleecy cloud, like a great many others, for in the hazy atmosphere its outline was not at all distinct.   I was not looking out for the moon, and so it was often a good while before I identified it as the moon.   I saw it simply as a bit of cloud floating about, along with many others of a like tissue, and even a like form.   At last it gradually distinguished itself from the rest by having always the same shape and the same place.   It got occasionally covered over or merged in the other fleecy things; but still it never failed to reassert its own individuality.   It was evidently a permanent thing amongst changeable things—an objective thing amongst subjective things, shall I say?   For I felt that these clouds were exhalations from myself (I being the earth), suggestions of my own mind, continually liable to change through the modifications which they suffered from other thoughts: they were all decidedly subjective.   At the same time they bore witness not unfrequently to the existence of an objective, just as the clouds bear witness to the existence of the sun by the glory which they receive from him. But I wanted and needed to have the consciousness of the actual presence of the great objective in me—not thoughts about Him, but Himself, or at least something which I was sure did not depend upon myself, but would always assert its own distinct independent reality, and which could not possibly be my own imagination, having this personal power and life in it, unmistakably." [1]

To give but one illustration more, in its way a masterpiece of expression, and like a portrait by Holbein, as fresh as if it had been penned yesterday. It is from the *Unconditional Freeness*. He is endeavouring to realise the perturbation of our first parent consequent upon the announcement of his pardon. The vivid portrayal of the scene, the swelling accumulation of horror as the picture unfolds itself before us, the tenderness that like a glittering thread runs through the web of remorse, are so powerful that no man can read the passage and be the same man afterwards.

" And although the Word of God is sparing of information with regard to the effect of the promise upon him, yet it is not inconsistent with the tenor of that information to hope and believe that he

[1] *Letters*, 265.

who was the first offender was also the first
monument of saving grace, and that with the
promise he received the Spirit of the promise and
the consolation of the promise into his soul.   For
surely never since has there been a created being
that has stood in such need of a strong consolation.
He had breathed the air of Eden, and had been
cast out—who has ever made such shipwreck?
He felt himself to be the author of a foul stain on
the universe of God.   He felt that his act was
irretrievable, that he had opened a floodgate which
he could not again shut, and through which a dark
tide rolled in, overwhelming all the destinies which
had been committed to his keeping.   He saw this
tide rolling in—he felt that it was his work, and
he could not stop it.   Verily he had need of a
strong consolation.   Who ever but he had his
conscience burdened with the ruin of a world—the
murder of an innumerable race of his own children.
He knew somewhat of the value of the light of
God's countenance, and he knew somewhat of the
horror of its loss; he had tasted the good and the
evil, and he felt that *his* heart and *his* hand had
done the deed which had severed unborn numbers
past numbering from the tree of life, and had
banished them from pleasant Paradise, their destined
place, and had made them outcasts from God and
wanderers through a homeless wilderness.   And

whereas he had been intrusted by God, for their behoof, with the pearl of eternal life, he had cast it from him, and instead of it had bequeathed to them the bitter cup of sorrow and death, and a proneness to every crime and an exposure to every misery. What a blow must Cain's murder have given to his heart, and what a fearful sense must it have given him of the living and growing and spreading reality of that curse which he himself had brought upon his offspring; and as his prophetic spirit went down that troubled stream of human life which was to issue from him, would not each drop lift up in the ear of his conscience an accusing voice against him; and as the various forms of outrage and calamity succeeded each other, would his heart not wither with the thought—' this is my work ' ? " [1]

[1] *Unconditional Freeness*, p. 108.

ERSKINE'S PECULIAR TEACHING

Calvinism, Old and New—What Benefits Christ secured for
all — Natural Law and Spiritual Truth — Erskine's
Mysticism and Universalism—The latter accounted for
and criticised—The True Place of Theology—Erskine's
Optimism.

BEFORE entering on a consideration of Erskine's
peculiar teaching, as that is to be found in his
published writings, including the posthumous
volume, *The Spiritual Order*, and his Letters,
it is necessary to recall the peculiar spiritual
forces at work at the time that he began to give
his views to the world. This is necessary in
order to understand that attitude of antagonism
to certain portions of the popular creed which he
felt compelled to adopt. First of all, then, there
was the influence of the school of Thomas Boston,
which was still powerful among the religious people
of Scotland, with its humbling estimates of human
nature, its uncompromising doctrine of divine
sovereignty, and its awful representations of the
divine wrath. On the other hand, there was the
leaven of Moderatism, enthusiastic only in its horror

of enthusiasm; its creed, grammar, and good
manners; its *summa bona*—cleverness, cheerfulness,
wine, and feasting. An element more wholesome
but less congenial to the soil than either of these
influences now precipitated itself in the form of
a great spiritual awakening that brought indeed a
welcome gospel to the land and captured some of
the finest minds in it. On the intellectual side,
however, the new Calvinism did not prove itself a
more satisfactory neighbour than the old had done.
It wore a look of benevolence, and apparently
brought blessings in its hand; but it soon turned
out that what it gave with the one hand it took back
again with the other. Professing a noble scorn for
systems fettered by the shackles of seventeenth-
century shibboleths, it really landed its own followers in the same remorseless entanglement of
logical contradictions. Announcing a message of
grace and truth for all without restriction or
qualifying condition, it really bestowed no benefit
on any man unless he were included within the
circle of the elect. Erskine did not believe in
this pseudo-liberalism any more than in the harsh
Calvinism it displaced. To him there was nothing
to choose between the two. Perhaps if anything
the harsher system was the preferable, being no
less gracious in its intentions to mankind, and a
great deal worthier of the character of the Divine

Being. Up to the last day of his life Erskine
never ceased to admire Calvinistic doctrine and to
believe in it, at least in so far as it made God
and the thought of Him all in all, while it made
the creature almost less than nothing and vanity,
thus engendering in the mind "a deep reverence,
a profound humility and self-abasement which are
the true beginnings of all religion." His restoration of the long-lost conception of Divine Fatherhood to evangelical teaching was not achieved
in the interests of maudlin sentimentality, nor
was it Fatherhood in its weak indulgence, but
Fatherhood in its majesty and strength which
received prominence in Erskine's teaching.

So far at one with Calvinism, he had no
liking for the Calvinism in vogue in his own
days. On the contrary, he had a deep distrust
of it, which was only equalled by the shame
he felt for the religion of Moderatism. He believed that nothing but infidelity could be the
consequence of holding it in the form in which it
was then believed, and therefore he maintained a
lifelong conflict with it. Probably he was not
any fairer to it than Wesley had been. Wesley
had imputed notions to his opponents that Scottish
Calvinism at least always repudiated, and that
were nothing short of frightful blasphemy.
Erskine objected most to all middle courses like

that of the Marrow theology, that were in his
view so many vain attempts to tone down the
decretum horribile. If there be a divine purpose
for mankind, its universality must either be something real or something nominal. If nominal only,
then the universal offer of benefits that are not
intended for all becomes a solemn farce, "inconsistent with the truthfulness and goodness of
God," an impossible creed which no honest man
can proclaim to his fellow - men. But neither
Wesley nor Erskine contented themselves with
being mere fault - finders. Both of them propounded positive views. They taught that the
benefits of grace, as they ought to be fully and
freely offered to mankind, are also intended for
mankind, and to a certain extent are really and
truly bestowed on mankind. "As through one
trespass the justification came unto all men to
condemnation, so through one act of righteousness
the free gift came unto all men to justification of
life." Erskine's interpretation of these words is,
that as every man has been born into an order
of sin, so every man is born into an order of
grace ; or, to put it otherwise, as Adam inflicted
on the world a sentence of death, so Christ has
brought a universal seed of life into the world
which is available for all those who do not reject
it. Erskine says in his book on Election :—

" If the character of the Fall be this, that one
offence by one man polluted the whole human
nature in the very fountain from which all its
streams flowed, and brought upon it a moral taint
and a condemnation to death which followed it
wherever it went, so that whether it appeared in
an infant or an idiot who had never exercised a
moral volition, or in a saint who had successfully
striven against its evil tendency, it still did tend
to sin, and carried along with it the sentence of
death, so that it was the unfailing token of weakness and sorrow and mortality to the creature who
partook in it,—if this be the character of the Fall,
I cannot think that any restoration or act of
grace could truly be said to meet such a calamity
unless it met the evil in all its streams as well as
in its fountain; that is, unless it put every individual, however much he had personally sinned
by yielding to the evil bent which had been thus
induced upon his nature, into a condition and
capacity of rising out of the Fall into a holiness
and blessedness equal to, if not beyond, what he
would have had on the supposition that the Fall
had never taken place.   And if there were foundation in fact and truth for any man fearing
that from any cause, and especially from his having
in past time yielded to the evil tendencies brought
on the nature by the Fall, he was really so shut

out from grace that the gift which has abounded
unto many is not permitted to abound to him; or
though it does abound to him, the capacity of
receiving it has been withdrawn from him; or that
though he may and does receive it, it may not
bring to him its saving, healing power, nor its seal
of the judicial award of eternal life: then the
apostle's boast is gone, and the triumph of evil in
the Fall is above the triumph of good in the
Restoration."

These views, thus eloquently, perhaps redund-
antly, expressed, seem to have held possession
of Erskine's mind as far back as 1828, but he
only expressed himself at that time in a tentative
manner in letters to private friends. Ultimately
he made an open avowal of his views, at first with
cautious reserve, as feeling the extreme difficulty
of the points at issue. But the belief grew more
and more deeply rooted within him, that whatever
use men might or might not make of the Christian
message, a *bôna fide* message of peace and goodwill
was addressed to them that embraced the whole
human race. Subsequently he saw reason—con-
sistently, as he thought, with the teaching of
Christ and of primitive Christianity—to advance
several steps further, and held that all the race
would ultimately be brought to believe the truth,
and so be saved.

Having broken from conventional ideas regarding the extent of the divine sacrifice for sin, it was inevitable that he should reconstruct his views on the nature of the great mystery. Scottish theology, believing in a limited Atonement, held the view that Christ was the Surety of a Mediatorial Covenant. Erskine, without altogether rejecting the federal theology, propounded a mystical theory of Christ's Divine Headship; according to which Christ suffered not as the substitute of some who were elected from all eternity, but in the capacity of Head and Representative of the race, a relationship which he held independently of the facts of sin and satisfaction. In setting forth this necessary and eternal connexion between Christ and humanity, Erskine is very happy in the metaphor he employs. Human nature, though composed of many members, is viewed in its totality as one organic body, of which Christ is the Head and Representative. To quote from *The Brazen Serpent*: "The whole nature is as one colossal man, of which Christ continues the Head during the whole accepted time and day of salvation." If we ask what were the benefits secured to our race absolutely and unconditionally through this eternal connection of Christ with it, his reply is, that the absolute and unconditional benefits are two in number,

namely, forgiveness and immortality. Again, to
those who fulfil the condition of faith, "this is the
great thing which Christ has accomplished by
suffering for us,—He has become a Head of new
and uncondemned life to every man in the light
of which we may see God's love in the law and
the punishment, and may thus suffer to the glory
of God and draw out from the suffering that
blessing which is contained in it."

Erskine disliked the ordinary ideas of substitution, and for the usual reasons, that the punishment of the innocent can never provide satisfaction
for the sins of the guilty; that such an idea
magnifies God's judicial, at the expense of His
Paternal, character; that it tempts us to look upon
the Saviour of the world rather as a refuge from
the Father, than as a way to Him; that it pre-
supposes the law to be a standard by which we are
to be tried and condemned, instead of one to which
it is the purpose of the Divine Being to raise us.
Not that he disallowed the claims of eternal Justice,
or supposed that even the Divine Being could
silence these claims by a mere act of will, or over-
step them. He held that we are bound to admire
the unsearchable wisdom and high principle "which
have combined the fullest mercy with the most
uncompromising justice." "We are not received
into the favour of God at all on the ground of our

own deservings, but on the ground of the satisfaction made to divine justice by the death of Christ as the Representative of sinners."

Erskine, it will be seen, makes more use of intuition than of logic in his studies and writings on theology. That being so, it would be unfair to carp at his frequently inconclusive logic. Once he said to a correspondent : " This view may be bad logic; that may pass with a friend: *I know it to be true.*" But what is strange is that he frequently seems to lose himself even on his own familiar ground. For example, he tells us that a universal and unconditional pardon is the true and essential teaching of Christianity. Believe the good news or disbelieve them, the pardon is ours. If we believe them, we get the good of the pardon here and now; we enjoy the tranquillising, purifying power of that gracious fact: but whether we do so or not, the pardon is a fact. Now, a practically minded thinker should not have become so confused on this subject, or spoken so much of pardon and so little of penitence as an inevitable condition or accompaniment of pardon. Erskine's doctrine would suit a world of Martin Luthers, a world of saints with the penitential murmur always on their lips, " Oh, my sin, my sin." But the real world, the world that Christianity has to capture, is a radically different place from the world in which Erskine apparently lived and moved and had his being. The problem to be faced is more difficult than he seems to have supposed. It does not consist in discovering how to bring consolation to the troubled conscience, but in knowing how to bring blind and erring consciences to a sense of their need.

One advantage Erskine thought he saw in his doctrine of unconditional forgiveness. He thought it guarded the mind from speculating about its faith, whether that were of the right sort. In a fine spirit of fervour he asks: "Do I believe in the Lord Jesus Christ? If I do, I am saved. If I do not, I am not saved! Then comes the question, Have I any evidence of the sincerity of my faith? . . . it is quite clear that the mind cannot find firm footing in this way. If a man draws his hope from this fact of his believing, he is as far from the spirit of the gospel as the man who rests his hope on his alms-deeds."

But though Erskine repels the intruder by the door, it actually comes in again by the window. On his own showing, he who would enter on the *full* blessedness of the gospel must do so by faith, as appears from the following quotation, and where is then his safeguard against the intrusion of un-comfortable speculations about faith being of the right kind? "The declaration of pardon through

Christ belongs to the whole world; but those only who believe this declaration have peace with God through it, that is, they only are justified, they only belong to the Church of Christ." " Again," he says, " a pardon unreceived can no more save the soul than a medicine unreceived can cure the body." The only real safeguard to be found is in adopting the Reformation doctrine of personal trust in a personal Saviour.

Probably nothing that Erskine has said, or could have said, on the profound problems in question is of pressing importance at the present day. We have other questions than those that troubled the generations who

> " reason'd high
> Of providence, foreknowledge, will, and fate,
> Fix'd fate, free will, foreknowledge absolute,
> And found no end in wandering mazes lost."

Nor has he, or others, said the last word that will be spoken on the doctrinal perplexities which they have helped to make a little less bewildering. But for Erskine this can be claimed, that he cleared the air of many nebulous notions that once darkened it, and that obscured the character of God. Limited and unlimited theories of grace are now happily a chapter of ancient history. They have given place, under such influences as his writings, to systems less scholastic and assertive,

less despairing and cruel, less removed from the
simplicity of Christ and of primitive Christianity.

Erskine, as we have seen, was not always logical,
yet in spite of his defective logic he had the
logician's liking for unity, for reducing the many
to the one.   It was this instinct of his intellectual
nature that made him press the analogy between
natural law and religious truth as far as he did.
According to him, the vital truths of the Christian
religion belong to the self-evident domain of exact
knowledge more naturally than to the circumstantial
world of historical testimony.   Christian truth has
come to us in conjunction with a series of historical
events.   The truths, however, are quite independent
of the facts, as much so as Kepler's laws of planetary
motion are independent of the movements of the
solar system.   As Christ in His day spoke to the
unthinking multitudes in parables, so positive
Christianity addresses the mass of humanity in
historical forms.   Spiritual Christianity, however,
is a religion of principles, which philosophy
might have been trusted to reach independently
of history had she followed the true path.   The
supernatural is the natural.   The Christ who appeared in time has always been in man's heart
speaking to him by the voice of conscience.   All
the moments in the history of Christ—the Incarnation, the Crucifixion, the Resurrection, the Ascen-

5

sion—are merely the outward manifestations of an inward universal experience. The truest incarnation takes place within ourselves. There the Lord of all suffers and dies, the just for the unjust, until He brings us to God.

In these flights into the realm of mysticism Erskine was seeking to satisfy the wants of his intellectual nature. He was seeking a foundation for the faith of Christianity more directly under his feet, and therefore more certain than the evidence of documents eighteen hundred years old. His spiritual cravings sent him in search of a Being whose presence was everlasting. It was the voice of evangelicalism addressing itself to him. Mysticism establishes Christ's reality after a similar fashion :

> " The cross of Golgotha thou lookest to in vain,
> Unless within thyself it be set up again."

" If thou believest that Christ was crucified for the sins of the world, thou must with Him be crucified to the same. If thou refusest to comply with this, thou canst not be a living member of Christ, nor be united to Him by faith. If thou believest that Christ is risen from the dead, it is thy duty to rise spiritually with Him. In a word : the birth, cross, passion, death, and resurrection of Christ *must, after a spiritual manner, be transacted in thee.*"

These might be the words of Erskine: they are those of the mystic John Arndt.

Erskine's mysticism is more rationalistic. He holds not merely that the Christ of history reproduces Himself in experience, but also that the Christ of experience explains and confirms the reality of the Christ of history. Questions of New Testament criticism that exercise so great a fascination now had small interest for him. With him, as with the mystics, inward experience is not everything, but it is the main thing,—and questions of history and criticism are not so vital as they are to the modern student of Christianity. Erskine would probably have gone as far as some in our own day who have said that it would be no *irreparable* loss were all the New Testament records lost, the experience of the saints afforded such abundant and incontestable evidence of Christ and Christianity. He drank so copiously from Law's fountain, that we need not wonder at his almost identifying natural and revealed religion. He reminds one forcibly of Lessing, who regarded the religion of Revelation as a schoolmaster to bring us to Christ, the true and inward Light and Life of men. According to Lessing, revealed Religion was merely a forestalment of truth, which the human mind, in the course of the ages, would have been capable of reaching unaided by inspiration from without. The

Bible was a primer, well suited for a young scholar ; but the time comes when he outgrows it, and must lay it aside. Lessing ignored the presence of any " moral dynamic " working from without, and reduced Christianity to the level of a system of ideas safely detachable from their source, and able to be securely planted within the mind of the race. Believers in historical Christianity, on the other hand, jealously guard even the intellectual elements of Revelation from hands like Lessing's and those who agree with him. They claim that even on its intellectual side there is more in the Christian revelation of God than has lain embryonically in the human mind from the beginning. If the Reformation doctrine of Holy Scripture be reasonable, that it pleased the Lord at sundry times and divers manners to reveal *not ourselves to ourselves, but Himself to us, and to declare His will to His Church*, it follows that ideas have been made known regarding God and His will that were not part of our original endowment, truths that man by searching could not find out.

There has always been a tendency to confound nature and the supernatural, and to merge the one in the other. The Hutchinsonians, in the eighteenth century, identified nature with the supernatural in a manner that now seems amusing. For example, they rejected the *Principia* of Newton, on the ground

that they were not formulated in the Bible; and
they encouraged old persons, who might have been,
one would suppose, better employed, to acquire a
knowledge of Hebrew roots and rabbinical dry-as-
dust lore, as if salvation depended thereon. Erskine
went to the other extreme, and confounded the
supernatural with the natural. He considered that
the great end and aim of a supernatural revelation
was to republish truths that were as old as creation,
truths that the world had lost sight of, to reinti-
mate to mankind those gracious relationships that
exist between the Creator and all His creatures,
and that have always existed, and to write large on
the statute-book of ethics those principles of the
fatherly Government of God that always have held,
and always shall hold sway. Every student of
Butler knows that Erskine, so far, was right; and
that a republication of the truths of natural religion,
and an authoritative sanction of them, was one of
the chief ends of a divine revelation.

" Christianity," says Butler, " is a republication
of and authoritative sanction to the truths of
natural religion. It instructs mankind in the
moral system of the world : that it is the work of
an infinitely perfect Being, and under His government; that virtue is His law; and that He will
finally judge mankind in righteousness, and render
to all according to their works in a future state ; and

which is very material, it teaches natural religion
in its genuine simplicity, free from those *superstitions* with which it was totally corrupted, and under
which it was in a manner lost."

Perhaps Erskine, in his tendency to one-sidedness, pushed the analogy between the supernatural
and the natural further than he ought to have
done. Sometimes he reminds us of one of the old
apologists, Justin or Aristides, *e.g.* who, in their
laudable endeavour to commend their religion to
the heathen world, represented it as in accordance
with reason and sound philosophy, as philosophy
brought within the reach of women and uneducated
men ; and did not emphasise its redemptive character.
Probably Erskine was rash in thus identifying
Scripture in all its parts with the natural government of the world and the teachings of man's
natural intuitions. But certainly he never denied
the reality of the supernatural, like the deists,
though he may have gone too far in identifying it
with the merely natural. It would be truer to
say that he exalted the merely natural into
supernatural rank. It is to be remembered, too,
that if the Christ of history appears in Erskine's
system a less important and indispensable figure
than in traditional theology, this is not because he
had any doubt or distrust of the historical. It is
because he regarded the person of the historical

Saviour as one with that mysterious Being who through countless ages has incarnated Himself within the life of humanity. He did no disparagement to the Christ who appeared in time, for us men and for our salvation. It is not that he valued the local and temporary in our religion less than other Christian teachers, but that he valued the eternal and the universal more.

Turning now to a consideration of Erskine's eschatological views, it is probably what he thought and taught on the terrible questions connected with the hope of a future life that has most interested and influenced other teachers. His views on the final destiny of mankind were revolutionary from the first. As early as the year 1827, when he was in his thirty-eighth year, and counted himself orthodox, judging from a remark about William Law's "unsoundness," he gives utterance to the hope of a final restoration of the race in several letters to private friends. "I have a hope," he says in one of these letters, "(which I would not willingly think contrary to the revelation of mercy) of the ultimate salvation of all." In another he says: "You know the universality of my hope for sinners. I hope that He who came to bruise the serpent's head, and to destroy the works of the devil, will not cease His labours of love till every particle of evil introduced into this world has been converted into good."

Eleven years later, in a letter in connexion with the death of a young kinsman, he talks with great confidence about life's education going on after death. Fourteen years afterwards (in 1853), when Frederick Denison Maurice was suspended from his chair in King's College, London, on account of his latitudinarian eschatology, Erskine writes to Lord Rutherfurd that he is in entire agreement with the teaching of his friend. " I congratulate him (Maurice, *i.e.*) on being a martyr in such a cause (*i.e.* the denial of the unending duration of future punishment), but I should be sorry if at this day the Church of England as a body confirms such a sentence. If spiritual perfection consists (as they would all admit it does) in the love of God and of men and of all righteousness, it is not easy to see how such a doctrine as the eternity of punishment can lead to it. Men cannot be frightened into love, and they cannot easily realise God as a God of love if such a doctrine be believed."

Still later (in the year 1864) he publishes his views at some length in a letter to Mr. Craig, who had given forth his views to the world. In Erskine's opinion the aim and end of punishment is remedial, and therefore it is wrong to think of it as endless.

He whose aim here and now in all our chastisement
is man's benefit must have the same benevolent
intention in all His future dealings with us, inasmuch as His purposes and character never change.
He based his confidence in the larger hope on the
revealed character of God, especially of the Divine
Fatherhood, and claimed the right to regard human
love and justice as similar to the divine, at least
as exemplified in the parental relation.   What
earthly parent, he asks, possessing even ordinary
power and goodness, would ever cease exerting
himself for the good of his children?   Again, it
was a corollary from the belief that education,
not probation, is the true interpretation of life,
that we should expect the ultimate recovery of
the whole family of mankind.   " The fiery trial
that is to try us must surely purify us at last, since
this is God's aim from the beginning,—not trial
ending in judgment, but education resulting in
perfection.   Who that sees life in the light of a
process of divine education; above all, that believes Christ to be the Educator within each
man, can contemplate the education ever ter-
minating, or the Educator ever abandoning, the
school ? "   " *He who waited so long for the forma-
tion of a piece of old red sandstone will surely wait
with much long-suffering for the perfecting of a
human spirit.*"

Principal Shairp, in his reminiscences, tells us, as an intimate personal friend, what he thought of Erskine's opinions on this terrible question.

"In one thing Mr. Erskine was altogether unlike most of those who hold the tenets of universalism. No man I ever knew had a deeper feeling of the exceeding evil of sin, and of the divine necessity that sin must always be misery. His universalistic views did not in any way relax his profound sense of God's abhorrence of sin. Anyone who talked intimately with Mr. Erskine in later years could not help hearing these views put strongly before him. Often when he urged them on me he seemed disappointed when I could not acquiesce. I used to urge that we do not know enough of the nature and possibilities of the human will to warrant us in holding that a time must come when it will yield to moral suasion which it may have resisted all through its earthly existence. Then as to the Bible, though there are some isolated texts which seem to make Mr. Erskine's way, yet Scripture, taken as a whole, speaks a quite different language. The strongest, most emphatic declarations against his views seem to be words of our Lord Himself. Therefore I shrink from all dogmatic assertions on this tremendous subject, desiring to go no further than the words of Scripture allow, till the day comes which shall bring forth His righteousness as the noon-day." [1]

While it is easy to agree with the sound state-ment of Principal Shairp, it is easy likewise to account for Erskine's attitude on this awful subject. We should remember the temptations he was under to revolt from the ideas current among the religious people of his time. The notions prevalent in his early days were worthy of the age of Tertullian. " You are fond of spectacles," exclaimed Tertullian, " expect the greatest of all spectacles, the last and eternal judgment of the universe. How shall I admire, how laugh, how rejoice, how exult when I behold so many proud monarchs and fancied gods groaning in the lowest abysses of darkness; so many magistrates who persecuted the name of the Lord, liquefying in fiercer fires than they ever kindled against the Christians; so many sage philosophers blushing in red-hot flames with their deluded scholars; so many celebrated poets trembling before the tribunal, not of Minos, but of Christ; so many tragedians more tuneful in the expression of their own suffering." [2]

Incredible as it may now appear, it is a fact that long after Erskine's time such pictures of the infernal regions continued to be placed before the people of Scotland by many evangelical divines,

[1] *Letters*, 526.   [2] Tertullian, *De Spectaculis*, c. 30.

though, to do the preachers justice, they did not
gloat over them as the African father appears to
do. Even the gentle Boston, *pastor pastorum*, had
spoken of the redeemed in heaven as rejoicing over
the tortures of the damned, and saying Hallelujah.
" The punishments," he says, "inflicted on the
greatest malefactors draw forth some compassion
from the spectators; but the damned shall have
none to pity them. God will not pity them, but
laugh at their calamity. The blessed company in
heaven shall rejoice in the execution of God's
righteous judgment, and sing while the smoke riseth
up for ever and ever." [1]   The godly M'Cheyne,
almost within earshot of Linlathen at the time that
Erskine lived and wrote, was startling congregations
out of their apathy by similar pictures. " What
good will it do you in hell that you knew all the
sciences in the world—all the events of history, and
all the busy politics of your little day ? Do you
not know that your very knowledge will be turned
into an instrument of torture in hell ? " [2]   In
another sermon M'Cheyne says : " The place in hell
is quite ready for every unconverted soul . . . . As
when a man retires at night to his sleeping-room,
so a place in hell is quite ready for every Christless
person. It is his own place. When the rich man

---

[1] *Fourfold State*, iv. 6.
[2] M'Cheyne's *Memoirs*, 303.

died and was buried, he was immediately in his
own place.   He found everything ready.   He lifted
up his eyes in hell, being in torments.   So hell is
quite ready for every Christless person.   It was
prepared long ago for the devil and his angels.
The fires are all quite ready and fully lighted and
burning." [1]   " Little children who are fond of your
plays, but are not fond of your coming to Jesus
Christ, who is the Saviour of little children, the
sword will come on you also.   Oh! it is a sore
slaughter that will not spare the young, nor the
lovely, nor the kind, the gentle mother and
affectionate child, the widow and her only son.
Should you then make mirth ?   Unconverted
families, when you meet in the evening to jest and
sport with one another, ask this one question,
Should we make mirth ?   Is your mirth reasonable ?
Is it worthy of rational beings ?   Unconverted
companions, who meet so often for mirth and
amusement, should you make mirth together when
you are in such a case ?   Ah! how dismal will
the contrast be when God says, Bind them in
bundles to burn them." [2]

Can we wonder at Erskine disliking such modes
of advancing religion, or blame him for heading a
revolt against them among those whom he had the
means of influencing ?   Or is it any cause for

[1] *Memoirs*, 321.   [2] *Ibid*. 323.

wonder that Boston's and M'Cheyne's successors to-day in the work of aggressive evangelicalism are so far of the same mind as Erskine himself, not indeed to the extent of accepting his universalism, but in the sense that they have now almost entirely abandoned the Tertullianism of a former time ?

Many causes have contributed to bring about this change. Physical science has contributed not a little. Under its influence the old material pictures of the future life have melted out of view. They have been insensibly put aside by the deeper questions which the new thought of the time has forced forward, especially the question whether there be a life to come at all. It is true that the challenge has been well met, but it is as true that those who have met it most successfully have usually left the issues raised by Erskine open. Tennyson, for instance, has done as much as any other teacher of the century to keep the hope of immortality alive in the minds of his countrymen. But he leaves the problem dealt with by Erskine open, or leans to the side of universalism.

Again, the awakening of the social conscience and the rise of humanitarian sentiments have done their part in toning down the harsh Tertullianism of a bygone time. Dark pictures of future judgment have faded out of the public mind, along with cruel treatment of the convict and the criminal classes.

A sense of solidarity and of social responsibility have sprung up within recent years that has greatly modified many of those ideas regarding individual responsibility that once prevailed both in Church and State.   There is now a disposition to make large allowance in the treatment of moral delinquency.   The contagion of bad example, the effects of unwholesome environment, the persistency of inherited taints are among the considerations that have compelled us to regard crime from a pathological as much as from a penal point of view, and in the light of these wider generalisations to recast and reconsider our ideas on the question of human guilt.

Then again, in the public teaching of religion the ethical element has had a place and prominence given to it which it could not have received in an earlier and a less educated period, and so modes of instruction like those of which we have given specimens are necessarily out of date.

It would indeed be foolish to ascribe the changes indicated to one set of causes only, as, for instance, to the teaching of writers like Erskine.   When progress is made, it will usually be found that many different causes, and not one only have contributed to bring it about.   So it has been in the case now under consideration.   Erskine was a single factor, but I think an important one, in toning down the harshness of former times. That has really been his work in this connexion, softening the asperities common in his time, and bringing into view many gracious elements of gospel truth that were too often ignored: that, rather than compelling assent to his dogma of universalism. Indeed, as the words of Principal Shairp show, he did not succeed in carrying his followers with him on the points made prominent in his eschatological creed. Nevertheless, he has surely done a great service in substituting moral and spiritual views of human destiny in place of the old penal and physical ones. It has been often said that sinners are not now afraid of God as they used to be—we have so inoculated them with the idea of the divine pity and love, and so toned down the idea of divine wrath and judgment; but probably that is a rash and hasty criticism. It is true, that the God of a departed materialism awes and restrains us no more. Worshippers come no more to the shrine of such a deity. But the God who eternally and unchangeably brings it to pass, that it goes ill with the wicked and well with the righteous, is still feared; and society is becoming more and more active and impartial in executing upon its delinquent members the decrees of that offended God.

In this chapter I have dealt with the contro-

versial elements in Erskine's teaching, and now
in conclusion must point out some things that rise
above the region of controversy, and that may commend him more to some as a teacher of religion.
In the first place, then, observe the important place
that is given to theology in his writings. He always
tries to give the subject of Christian doctrine an
expression as clear, as convincing, and as spiritual
as it can receive. Evidently he had no fondness
for a merely practical Christianity, and little
sympathy with those—now happily a diminishing
number—who wildly declaim against creeds as
containing a mixture of metaphysics and dogma
entirely foreign to the Christianity of the Gospels.
He held, on the contrary, that no teacher of the
Christian religion was worthy of the name who
should refuse to give the fullest explanation possible
of the meaning of Christ's claims and redemptive
work, and of the experiences and testimony of His
followers. In other words, the science of theology
is bound to receive its due place of importance
because of the necessary laws of the human mind,
and must also be dogmatic and metaphysical. It
is thus interesting to see that the signs of a revived
interest in the subject of Christian doctrine, that
are so apparent in the theological activity of the
present day, are fully anticipated throughout
Erskine's work.

6

In another respect he came into vital touch
with present-day problems. He believed in theology,
as we have seen, but not only so, he also considered it the duty of the theologian to see well to
it that the credentials of Christianity rested on
foundations from which neither criticism nor
philosophy could dislodge them. In our day
criticism has undoubtedly aided and enriched faith
to a large extent, but it has also subjected faith to
many severe trials; and external authorities that
once commanded respect are no longer submitted
to. We have been compelled by the force of
circumstances to go in search of witnesses whose
evidence could stand all tests, and we have found
these in a quarter where they have all along
existed, namely, in the inward witness of the Holy
Spirit to the truth of Revelation. Now, it was one
of the chief tasks which Erskine set before him in
his writings, to direct attention to the inward
testimony of the Spirit to revealed truth. Thus
he says in his latest book: "I do not say that man
could, without an external revelation, have arrived
at that knowledge of God which is communicated
in the Scriptures,—for, indeed, the history of the
efforts of the human mind contradicts such a
thought, but that after the communication has
been made he can perceive its coherency and
reasonableness, even to the length of seeing that it

must be so, and could not be otherwise, and that though he owes his first sight of divine truth to the outward authority, he may come to hold it as a possession of which no questioning or shaking of the outward authority can rob him." [1]

Erskine makes another contribution towards the solution of present-day difficulties. There is a well-known phase of unbelief at the present time that we may describe in a popular sense as utilitarian. I mean the unbelief of those who tell us, sometimes with a mournful pathos, that they find in Christianity no succour, no really serviceable benefit, no answer to the cry, "Who will show us any good?" The difficulty of these objectors is not with regard to the truthfulness of Christianity as a supernatural religion, but merely with regard to its helpfulness and usefulness in the practical affairs of life. If the gospel really helped them in their struggles with life, and in the working out of their life-problems, the question of miracles and of Christ's unique claims would never for a moment interfere with their acceptance of His religion. They admire His teaching and they revere His Person, but they find the gospel of no use to them in the battle of life; they can manage to live as well without it as with it. We have here a complaint frequently brought against Chris-

[1] *The Spiritual Order*, p. 79.

tianity by the democracy of the present day. Doubtless the complaint may be in great measure unreasonable and unwarranted; nevertheless, it exists and influences masses of people who never give it any articulate expression. Now, I am not aware that Erskine anywhere notices the complaint, or directly address himself to it, but his writings are full of instruction regarding the helpfulness and indispensableness of Christianity to the right ordering of human life. In his view, the revelation of the personality and love of God, the reality of a spiritual order in the government of the world, the education of the soul by experience of sanctified suffering, and the consciousness of eternal life, bringing with it the hope of life hereafter, constituted a gospel for mankind sufficient to make the poorest life rich and the meanest lot great. Erskine tried to make men see that the gospel, despite all circumstances, was something wonderfully fitted to cheer, to uplift, to satisfy. Dr. Hanna tells us that he was in the habit of sending a copy of the late Archbishop Trench's verses to his friends, and it will be seen that they sum up, in simple, brave words the message which he delighted to deliver :

> "I say to thee, do thou repeat
> To the first man thou mayest meet,
> In lane, highway, or open street,

That he and we and all men move
Under a canopy of love,
As broad as the blue sky above.

And ere thou leave him, say thou this
Yet one word more—they only miss
The winning of that final bliss

Who will not count it true that love,
Blessing, not cursing, rules above,
And that in it we live and move.

And one thing further make him know—
That to believe these things are so,
This firm faith never to forego,

Despite of all that seems at strife
With blessing, all with curses rife,
That *this* is blessing, *this* is life."

ERSKINE'S LETTERS

A Treasury of Consolation—Erskine's Qualifications—The
Outspokenness of the Letters—The Scottish Coleridge—
Letter to Lord Rutherfurd—Social Life of Scotland—
Prophecy, Popery, Phrenology—Letter to Dr. Chalmers
from Rome—Popular Rights—Extracts—The Gospel of
Lucretius ; the Laughter of Socrates—Calvinism, Circum-
stances, Freedom, etc.

ERSKINE'S reputation rests on his skill as a letter-
writer, rather than that of a writer of books.
Literature has usually been produced when the
authors have been least conscious of producing it.
Samuel Rutherfurd, famous in his day as a preacher,
scholar, ecclesiastic, theologian, is only known now
as the author of a collection of letters written
without premeditation. His Letters are remembered, and his *Disputatio Scholastica de Divina
Providentia* is forgotten, because the one is
experience and the other dialectics. It has been
with letters as with psalms and hymns. "There is
almost no heresy in the hymn-book," says the late
Henry Ward Beecher. "In hymns and psalms we
have a universal ritual. It is the theology of the
heart that unites men. Our very childhood is

embalmed in sacred tunes and hymns. Our early
lives and the lives of our parents hang in the
atmosphere of sacred song. The art of singing
together is one that is for ever winding invisible
threads about persons." Erskine, then, is likely
enough to be remembered as a writer of letters
after his work as a theologian has been forgotten.
Being a lay theologian, and not a clergyman, he
was answerable for his peculiar views neither to
court nor council. Ordinary ecclesiastics therefore
could afford to ignore him—as they foolishly
thought, or dismiss him from their consideration
as a blind leader of the blind. Some of the fierier
sort openly denounced him, and could have con-
signed his books and perhaps himself also to the
common hangman to be burned. But others, like
Dr. Chalmers, though they differed from him on
many material points, were proud of his friendship
as long as they lived. Without doubt his personal
character was most attractive, even saintly, and
ecclesiastics, although they might dislike his teaching, could not refrain from revering the man. It is
an interesting fact that at the present day churches
that cannot tolerate Erskine's theological ideas
prescribe his Letters to their students as a text-
book in practical religion. These Letters compose
the largest and most delightful volume of all his
writings, revealing, as they do, the working of a

remarkable spiritual genius. It is from them that we gather the truest and most authentic biography of the man. In living portraiture they set forth the finest rendering of "the Christian" that the nineteenth century has produced. They introduce us to the life of a devout seer who has made the world better and brighter for all other men. They conduct us across the threshold of his home-life, and we mingle among groups of guests within this consecrated circle, with whom to mingle is as sacramental wine to the soul.

The Letters have many remarkable qualities. For one thing, they constitute a treasury of consolation that must have seemed most opportune at the time of their first appearance, and that is sure to increase in value as the years come and go. Calls to the unconverted and tracts addressed to the worldly have been supplied in abundance, but a writer who could communicate consolation to the unhappy has appeared seldom. The writer possessed many qualifications for the task of consoler. He had had his own great share of sorrow. "As I look back on my own life, I find all the most remarkable epochs marked by the deathbeds of those whom I loved." Again, his doctrine of the larger hope gave him a powerful advantage over other men in his office of consoler. It enabled him to administer solid and definite

From a Photograph by

Linlathen House.

J. Valentine & Son, Dundee.

comfort to those most acutely distressed, not mere
crumbs of comfort or counsels of patience and
resignation. He was, however, principally indebted
to his own native largeness of heart for the possession
of this useful talent. It was that which qualified
him so well to be a true priest to down-hearted
men and women. He was endowed naturally with
the fine gift of fellow-feeling, and this it was that
made him win for himself the fame of having been
the first to render humanity and Christianity most
completely into the form of sympathy. Nor did
he feel for those only who belonged to his own
select social circle, or merely relieve suffering by
the application of spiritual opiates. Like a true
physician of the soul, he always tried to heal the
heart that was smitten, as well as calm and soothe
it. I doubt whether Erskine could have raged at
anything in this world even if he had tried, but he
came as near doing it as he could when he met
with frothy sentiment. "The entire want of
theology provokes me," he once said. His Letters,
as we might expect, are healthy, invigorating
reading, unlike the usual productions of pietistic
writers. He never puts on airs, never patronises
men, never propounds the impossible, never leaves
the impression of unreality. All is written
in a spirit of love, of manliness, of a sound
mind.

Another remarkable feature of the Letters is their outspokenness on the subject of personal religion. Such outspokenness has seldom been common even among religiously minded people They have often shrunk from explicitness on the delicate matters of the soul through an honest dislike to being regarded upsetting and presumptuous. " What is your religion ? " Dr. Johnson was once asked.—" The religion of every sensible person, to be sure," was the reply. " And what religion may that be ? "—" Every sensible person keeps that to himself, sir." Some time ago Mr. W. T. Stead asked a number of notabilities to name any hymns that had helped them in the religious life. Among those who were asked the question was Lord Rosebery, who said in reply : " I decline to confess to the public in general on such a subject as this." The reply was probably natural and proper enough in the circumstances, but without doubt we would all be the better of laying to heart Mr. Stead's words of reproof. " There is a curious—and not very creditable—shrinking on the part of many to testify as to their experience in the deeper matters of the soul. It is an inverted egotism—selfishness masquerading in disguise of reluctance to speak of self. Wanderers across the wilderness of life ought not to be chary of telling their fellow-travellers where they found the green oasis, the healing spring, or the shadow of a great rock in a desert land. It is not regarded as egotism, when the passing steamer signals across the Atlantic wave, news of her escape from perils of iceberg or fog, or welcome news of good cheer. Yet individuals shrink into themselves, repressing rigorously the fraternal instinct which bids them communicate the fruits of their experience to their fellows. Therein they deprive themselves of a share in the communion of saints, and refuse to partake with their brother of the sacramental cup of human sympathy, or to break the sacred bread of the deeper experiences."[1]

Probably it did not require any great courage on Erskine's part to speak out prophet-like of God and for God in every private letter that he wrote, even to lovers of silence like Carlyle. Probably it came quite easy to him. His mind was saturated with the thought

> " That he and we and all men move
> Under a canopy of love
> As broad as the blue sky above."

And so he hastened to tell the good news wherever he could, and to whomsoever. It is strange that this gift of tongues, as we may call it, has been given so seldom to men, or at least that so few have been able to use it so as to recommend and

[1] *Hymns that have helped*, 3.

not rather retard religion. Erskine has been called the Scottish Coleridge. The likeness is not very striking, though there is a likeness. He was not an omnivorous reader like Coleridge, or outside his own special province a particularly clear or well-informed thinker. Again, he was more of a traveller than Coleridge, and nourished the imaginative sense on the glories of Italian art. But he was distinctly like Coleridge in respect to the gift of communicativeness, which is as marked a feature of his correspondence as it was of his conversation. Like Coleridge, he was readily communicable, though the themes on which he was readiest to speak were those on which the great talker was usually reserved; and although he never ceased to have the truest regard for the company of poor men—for the courier who travelled with him over the Alps, and for the humble shepherd of his own Scottish glens —he drew to him the finest spirits of his time, as Coleridge had also done, as to the shrine of an oracle. Vinet and he had many points in common. Vinet considered it insulting to those higher relationships which we hold to one another not to converse freely on the things that concern us most deeply. We ought not to treat Christianity as if it were "*a dead friend* whose name is not to be mentioned for fear of reawakening bitter regrets." Erskine seems always to have felt the obligation to speak on the highest things, and this he does readily and with a charming naturalness, not to his female friends only, and pietistic men folks, but with people of fashion,—friends at the bar and on the bench, men of the calibre of Carlyle and Mackenzie, son of "the Man of Feeling." Take this letter to Lord Rutherfurd, on the death of his wife, in illustration of the obligation referred to :—

" Is your heart finding any rest ? I should be so thankful of a word from you to let me know in what state you are. There was something fearfully stunning and overwhelming in the suddenness of the blow at last, notwithstanding her long delicacy. My dear friend, I know no man who has had to pass through such varied trials as you—none to whom the voice from above has come in such different languages, such sorrow and such success ; and if in your present circumstances I had room in my heart for any other prayer for you than that you might be supported and comforted, I would ask that that oft-repeated voice might not come to you in vain. Our spiritual nourishment here, on this pilgrimage, is broken body and shed blood, a will of God revealed in a blighted will of men." [1]

A week later he writes as follows—the date is 30th October 1852 :—

[1] *Letters*, 158.

"Who is living with you, and how are you occupying yourself? I ask this not with the wish that you could find something to withdraw you from your sorrow, but rather hoping that you may be learning its true use. We are placed amongst dying things that we may be forced to take hold of the undying, and to discover that this ' undying ' is a Person with whom it is possible to have fellowship, and from whom we may derive help and consolation, which is certainly our highest learning. ' Come unto Me, all ye that are weary and heavy laden, and I will give you rest,' is the utterance which He addresses to us in all the variety of our circumstances; not calling us from other things, but teaching us to find Him in them all." [1] . . .

Erskine's mind was cast in an ethereal mould. It moved in a high celestial orbit. And yet for one of his stamp, whose conversation and correspondence turned so naturally to religious themes, there is a delightful absence of all morbid tendencies, all gloomy asceticism, all offensive language. He never despises the creature, never disparages the world, never does violence to the natural affections, never undervalues the good gifts of Heaven. He is saved from all these extravagances by two things: first, by his healthy feeling for Nature, at whose abundant fountains he imbibed joy and living

[1] *Letters*, 159.

water ; and secondly, by his keen enjoyment of human friendship. He loved his friends, — he had friends worthy of his love,—and from the affection that was natural and human he learned the preciousness of the love which is heavenly and divine.

The Letters have another, although a secondary, importance besides that of their elevated spiritual tone, which constitutes their chief value. They afford us, as almost all letters do, some glimpses at the social life of the times. The politics, the literature, the ecclesiastical ferments, the faddisms of half a century ago and more are seen in the Letters,—not, indeed, as a diary or an autobiography would have served them up, seasoned with spicy tit-bits and tattle, but still pleasant and palatable enough to the taste, though bare and wanting in details, as perhaps letters must necessarily be. We come across evidence of the spiritual barrenness which early in the century characterised the religious life of the time, and of which Macaulay, in his essay on Bunyan, gives so striking an illustration, when he says that Cowper confessed that he dared not name John Bunyan in his verses for fear of moving a sneer. Erskine and others bear an indirect testimony to this torpid state of religious life when they cordially hail, as the sign of better times, the appointment of Dr. Chalmers to a theological professorship in 1827. " Dr. Chalmers is appointed to the Divinity Chair in the Edinburgh University. May the Lord bless His work in the hand of His servant." We see similar signs of religious stagnation in the fact that people in Erskine's position find the society they crave not at home, but in Geneva and Paris, as the Reformation preachers so often found in earlier times. Turning to particular phases of life, we see how popery, prophecy, and phrenology stirred the public mind half a century ago. Pious people made a study of the prophecies, and lived in daily expectation of a great crisis. Popery they regarded as the great falsehood foretold in Scripture, which only deceived those who wish to be deceived, and yet somehow cannot be suppressed. And Mr. Combe went up and down the country "reading" people's heads, and slyly humouring the Tories of the old school, pointing out the redundant combativeness and destructiveness of the Irish as an argument against the extension of the franchise to Ireland. Such were among the occupations of our grandfathers and grandmothers as they are reflected in the correspondence of Thomas Erskine. Speaking of the study of prophecy reminds us of a letter to Dr. Chalmers in 1827 from Rome, in which, among other interesting things, Erskine gives an amusing account of a Catholic priest, for whom the study of prophecy had a great fascination.

"I am quietly looking upon the seat of the Beast, and wondering at him, at the manner of his existence, and at his duration. I have met here with Irving's book upon the Prophecies. I don't suppose that any mere interpreter of prophecy has ever before assumed such a tone of confidence and authority. I am a little surprised that the fate of former interpreters has not warned him. He is scarcely meek enough. He seems to intend to brave and insult such of his readers as hesitate about yielding their entire consent; but it is a magnificent book, full of honest zeal. There is a Romish priest here who in the reign of the last Pope wrote a book on the Prophecies, in which the year 1830 is fixed as the termination of all the wrath. He carried his MS. to the regular licenser, who showed it to the Pope before granting leave to publish. The Pope desired that licence should be given him to publish it in the year 1831. I have an Italian master who is a true, honest believing Catholic, and who cordially pities the souls of the Protestants. He tells me that the study of the Prophecies here is becoming much more general than formerly, and that there are many expecting a great crisis.

"I am almost a believer in the nearness of the end, and I like to encourage in myself any idea

7

which leads to watchfulness and prayer, and which gives a greater prominency to spiritual and eternal objects. I desire to look and wait for the coming of the Lord, and to long for His appearing. I wish you were here for a month now, instead of making your usual tour. The Niobé of nations is a happy name for Rome. She is full of beauty and interest and sorrow, but there is a lie in her right hand. I have met with some good specimens of Christianity from our own country here at Rome. I have never yet seen a Catholic who was deeply spiritually minded. I have not found any in the style of à Kempis: they are formalists even when they are honest believers, which is not a very usual thing amongst the tolerably educated classes, and never at all in France. The functions of the Holy Week are just over,—and such mummery to be sure! and then the celebration of Easter by an illumination! The existence of such a system, ecclesiastical and political, is a fact as unaccountable, or more so, than the continued separate preservation of the Jews,—the government of a corporation of priests submitted to during the military turbulency of the Middle Ages and the enlightened revolutionary scepticism of the present day, and a system of imposition, and which imposes on no one and is yet opposed by no one." [1] . . .

[1] *Letters*, 31.

Erskine's political sympathies were of the fine old Conservative order, and the incoming tide of popular rights caused him deep searchings of heart, that make his Letters wholesome reading at the present day. Writing in 1843, he says : " All through Europe the lower classes of the people have learned that they have rights ; but they have not yet learned that the real political good of man is to be well-governed and not self-governed. They suppose that these two things are one. The gospel that they would desire is, Every man his own king ; and that other gospel which is next neighbour to it, Every man his own God : whereas the true gospel is, You are not your own, but bought with a price." [1]   Later, in 1866, when he was seventy-seven, he writes : " I trust it may please God to scatter those Fenian raiders, and to use them as inducements for men to take refuge under the shadow of His wings.   Our country is in a strange state.   This Reform Bill seems like the breaking down of barriers so as to allow the rush of all disorders.   We want wisdom to govern us, not numerical majorities.   True liberty consists in being delivered from our own vain passions and appetites and selfish will, and it would seem that many now think that liberty consists in the indulgence of these things, and that the restraint

[1] *Letters*, 132.

of these is slavery."[1] . . . Writing at the time
of the Disruption to James Mackenzie, he says: "I
have been reading Carlyle's *Past and Present*, out of
which two elements he rears a horoscope of the
future. He thinks that our great want is that of a
true aristocracy,—a strong, intelligent domineering
aristocracy in its two forms of governing and
teaching. We need men who will 'mak' us for
to know it,' like Sir Harry, and who will also
'mak' us for to do it.' These are our great
desiderata, and he seems to hope much from
men coming to be sensible that these are our
needs."[2] . . .

I conclude this chapter with extracts from the
Letters :—

THE GOSPEL OF LUCRETIUS

"It was a curious gospel that Lucretius preached
to the Romans of his time, 'There are no gods,'
—*hurrah!* and yet it was a real gospel in his
mind. He meant to tell them that in the government of the universe there was no caprice nor
favouritism,—no selfish seeking for honours or
sacrifices, no malice nor jealousy to be gratified,
no Venus, nor Mars, nor Juno who ruled the affairs
of men for their own private views and piques
and interests, and not on any general principle

---

[1] *Letters*, 217.   [2] *Letters*, 129.

of good,—but fixed, eternal laws of justice and righteousness. I have a great sympathy with the old poet, and am sure that he would have welcomed a fuller gospel if it had been suggested to him,— a gospel declaring that not inexorable laws, however just and righteous, but a Being whose righteousness is love, guides and rules the universe, and that His one unchangeable purpose in creating and sustaining man is to make Him a partaker in His own blessedness by making him a partaker in His own righteousness, and that all the events of life, the infinite variety and complication of joys and sorrows and duties and relations, in which we find ourselves involved, constitute the education by which He would train and lead us to that great consummation." [1]

THE LAUGHTER OF SOCRATES

" Both Socrates and Voltaire laughed, but what different laughs ! Voltaire thought of nothing but of pulling down what was wrong, and he did so much really good and useful work in this way that he did not feel the necessity of building up. He was satisfied with negation : that is to say, negation with him was so active an employment that he did not come to feel that in itself it is a vacuum and can satisfy no one. There is something

[1] *Letters*, 215.

irresistibly comical in the levity with which he
treats the gravest principles,—it is like a child
pulling off an old man's wig; whereas dear Socrates
has such a deep and true veneration for everything that is really right in principle, he feels that
without it man and the universe are nothing more
than a dust-storm." [1]

CALVINISM

" When we see one part of a truth generally
overlooked we are disposed to become its
champions, and, like the old knights, to claim
from all the world the acknowledgment that it is
best and fairest.   The Wesleyans have been
generated by Calvinism, of which they are the
supplement.   Calvinism, by what I cannot but
think a very absurd misconception of the meaning
of the 7th chapter of the Epistle to the Romans,
teaches that a man may be in a safe state and
may be a true believer whilst he continues carnal
and sold under sin according to the 14th verse.
The Wesleyans, seeing the evil of this, have set
up their doctrine of perfection, which is certainly
true in the main, for a man may hold fast the
grace of God, and that grace is sufficient to keep
him from evil, but their statements of it are not
always wise or right." [2]

[1] *Letters,* 155.   [2] *Letters,* 113.

On Blaming Circumstances

" When we feel pain or uneasiness in our bodies we naturally refer it to some internal malady, and we look out for a remedy which may remove it. But when we feel pain or uneasiness in our minds, we are disposed to refer it, not to any malady in the mind itself, but to the circumstances in which we are placed, and thus men are employed rather in attempting to change their circumstances than in endeavouring to cure their souls." [1]

Freedom

" The idea of a sorrowing God shocks the minds of many. It does not shock mine: I cannot conceive love being without sorrow. I cannot believe that man can give me a sympathy which God does not give me : I cannot believe that man can give me a sympathy which does not flow into him from God ; and if anyone should say to me, Why does an omnipotent God bring creatures into existence who grieve themselves and cause grief to Him ? I answer, God, in making men, made creatures whom He desired to be good ; goodness means choosing to be good : they cannot be made good, they must choose it, and omnipotence cannot do that without unmaking the man ; wise and

[1] *Letters*, 131.

loving training must do it. God desires the joy of seeing His creatures choose to be good, and the capacity of choosing to be good implies the capacity of refusing to be good, and thus the possibility of such a joy is always accompanied with the risk of a great sorrow, which sorrow, I believe, God knows and feels." [1]

PERSONAL PROVIDENCE

"What a blessed and glorious thing human existence would be if we fully realised that the infinitely wise and infinitely powerful God loves each one of us with an intensity infinitely beyond what the most fervid human spirit ever felt towards another, and with a concentration as if He had none else to think of." [2]

PERSONAL RELIGION

"Happy the heart that has learned to say *my* God! All religion is contained in that short expression, and all the blessedness that man or angel is capable of.[3] . . . All religion is in the change from He to Thou. It is a mere abstraction as long as it is He. Only with the Thou we know God." [4]

[1] *Letters*, 249.   [2] *Letters*, 253.   [3] *Letters*, 36.   [4] *Letters*, 359.

THE MACLEOD CAMPBELL CASE

The Macleod Campbell Case—The Manifestation of Spiritual
Gifts.

THERE is nothing to wonder at, and not very much
to complain about, in the fact that Erskine's life
was not fuller of events and yields us so little
biographical material. His existence, it must be
remembered, was so considerable an event to his
country and to the cause of religion generally,
that the quiet, uneventful routine in which he
seems to have passed the most of his long life was,
after all, a most fitting and natural enough thing.
To the outside world who did not know him he
was a reserved person, a dreamer of dreams, a
man who held peculiar views, and nothing more.
The chronicles certainly are far from plentiful,
but they are not quite bare. Among other things
we may note that Erskine was a traveller at a
time when continental travel was not as common
as it is now; and as he was no idle traveller, but
one who saw all that was to be seen and met
everybody who was of any consequence, his letters

from abroad are still as fresh and full of interest
as any that we can read. Another " compartment "
of life, to use an expression of his own, that is
worth looking into, is that wonderful succession
of visitors that came year by year to Linlathen—
Carlyle, Charles Kingsley, Dean Stanley, Jowett—
and the manner of their entertainment there,
intellectually, spiritually, and otherwise, such as
no other Scottish laird before or since has ever
laid before his guests. But passing by these
inviting " compartments," let us speak of two
matters that caused a great stir in their time and
that Erskine took the liveliest interest in. One
of them was the case of Dr. John Macleod Campbell of Row, whose acquaintance he made quite
unexpectedly shortly after the publication of *The
Unconditional Freeness*. The eventful meeting
took place in a church in Edinburgh where Campbell was officiating, and where, to Erskine's great
delight, he heard him expound certain gracious
aspects of gospel truth not often heard at the
time, and that entirely corresponded with his own
views. Coming out of church in great excitement,
he remarked : " I have heard to-day from that
pulpit what I believe to be the true gospel."
Erskine from that day took the young preacher to
his heart as a chosen vessel, and stood by him up
to the end, amid all the fiery trials through which

he passed.   In those days in Scotland, as everyone
knows, good men thought nothing of travelling
long distances on foot to hear a favourite preacher
and listen to a true gospel sermon.   Erskine, in
the spirit of his pious countrymen, now took up
his residence at the Gareloch for several months in
the summer, in order to be near his young friend
and profit by his ministrations and fellowship.
We need not go into the history and merits of the
Macleod Campbell case.   Suffice it to say that
Erskine followed the case throughout with the
deep concern of one who beheld in his friend a
martyr for Christ and Christian truth.   At the
meeting of the church Court at which Campbell
was made to repeat the offending discourse, Erskine
was present as an interested auditor of the pro-
ceedings.   He was present also at the meeting of
the supreme Court when the blow fell.   There a
strange thing happened which drew from him a
witty repartee.   The principal clerk of Assembly
having been appealed to in reference to a question
of procedure, declared in the excitement of the
moment—meaning, of course, quite the reverse—
that "these doctrines of Mr. Campbell would
remain and flourish after the Church of Scotland
had perished and was forgotten."   Upon hearing
this strange statement, Erskine leaned back and
whispered to those behind him, "This spake he

not of himself, but being High Priest,—he prophesied."

Another movement that greatly interested Erskine was the remarkable manifestation of gifts at Port-Glasgow and the Gareloch about the year 1830. The excitement had spread so far that people were coming all the way from London to witness the movement. Erskine went to Port-Glasgow and stayed for six weeks in the house of the brothers Macdonald, the two outstanding recipients of the alleged gifts. Multitudes of people, of course, treated the whole matter as an outburst of religious fanaticism. But the high character of the chief *dramatis personæ* made it impossible for that view to become general. Accordingly, many people, of whom Erskine confessed himself one, believing that there are more things in heaven and earth than are dreamed of in our philosophy, lent a willing ear to all well-authenticated reports of the movement that happened to reach them. Erskine, as I have said, went to see and judge for himself on the spot. His appetite for spiritual knowledge was like another man's thirst for gold. The Macdonalds were respectable but peculiar men, shipbuilders on the Clyde. It was said that they fasted and practised other austerities, and that the only book that they read was the Bible.

It was said, too, that before closing the yard in the evening they convened their workmen together for prayer, and that because they did this they did not deem it necessary to insure the place against fire. Whether these things were so or not, they were unquestionably men of high character and pure motive. Many things about them confirm us in this view. Thus, at the time of the cholera visitation, they went about among the victims of that awful scourge, attending to their wants with a courage and a zeal that astonished their fellow-townsmen. Again, when they received an offer from the Irvingite Church in London, in recognition of their wonderful prophetic gifts, "not seeing the hand of God in the matter," they declined the call, notwithstanding the fact that it came to them at a time when they were experiencing serious business difficulties, and meant comfortable provision for the rest of their lives. When it is remembered also that they were modest, unpretentious men who never dreamed of placing their own gifts, inspired by the Holy Ghost, as they believed them to be, on a par with the authority of the written Word, as men with such beliefs have often been tempted to do; that they were rigid Sabbatarians and were free from every kind of Antinomian taint; and, most wonderful of all, that they so disliked schism that even after

the clergy of the district began in their own
presence to preach at them from the pulpit, they
still attended the services of the Church and
remained loyal to her, it will be seen that they
were men whom good people felt bound to love
and admire.   Erskine liked them for these
qualities and for the liberal theology of their
teaching.   It leaned to the side of his own
gracious Calvinism; it knew nothing of limited
theories of the Atonement; it gave a new prominence, as he also did, to the doctrine of the
Incarnation.   When he visited the Macdonalds he
was profoundly impressed by the things which he
saw and heard among them.   At the meetings
which he attended he saw rustics, known to possess
neither musical nor linguistic gifts, seized suddenly
with a holy frenzy, break forth into prolonged and
mysterious utterances, sometimes in a tone of pre-
ternatural loudness, and sometimes in the stately
measure of anthem music.   Meanwhile the bewildered audience saw something in the speaker's
countenance like the look of prophetic rapture.
What did it all mean ?   Of what world could this
be the language ?   There was no human speech
like it.   Could it be the language of heaven, the
speech of the angels ?   It might, it must be so.
And if it were mostly unintelligible, did not that
indicate that its character was eucharistic, not

evangelistic, a language addressed to God and not
to man ?

Verbatim reports of these mysterious utterances
were never taken, though specimens of the ordinary
kind are preserved in the Macdonalds' Memoirs.
The leaders of the movement discouraged the practice of reporting. James Macdonald, indignant at
some who made the attempt, held up Erskine's
conduct in the matter in contrast with theirs.
" How unlike Mr. Erskine, who said, ' I felt so much
of the Spirit's presence that I marked none of the
words. I knew the voice of God in it, and that
satisfied me.' " This discouragement of reporting
the Tongues was the reverse of discreditable to the
Macdonalds and their friends. They were against
bringing any writing into existence that might be put
into opposition with the Bible. Indeed, they quar-
relled with the Irvingites on this very point, the latter
insisting on putting the Tongues before the Bible.

Erskine at first formed a high opinion of the
movement, and of those most closely identified with
it, and for a long time approved of it and supported
it out and out. But later on he felt compelled to
change his view, and to dissociate himself from the
movement, and in an appendix to his book on Election, published in 1837, he thus explained himself :—

" In two former publications of mine, the one

entitled *A Tract on the Gifts of the Spirit*, the other,
The Brazen Serpent, I have expressed my conviction
that the remarkable manifestations which I witnessed in certain individuals in the West of Scotland, about eight years ago, were the miraculous
gifts of the Spirit, of the same character as those
of which we read in the New Testament. Since
then, however, I have come to think differently,
and I do not now believe that they were so.

"But I still continue to think that to anyone
whose expectations are formed by and founded on
the declarations of the New Testament, the disap-
pearance of those gifts from the Church must be a
greater difficulty than their reappearance could
possibly be.

"I think it but just to add that though I no
longer believe that those manifestations were the
gifts of the Spirit, my doubts as to their nature
have not at all arisen from any discovery or even
suspicion of imposture in the individuals in whom
they have appeared. On the contrary, I can bear
testimony that I have not often in the course
of my life met with men more marked by native
simplicity and truth of character, as well as by
godliness, than James and George Macdonald, the
two first in whom I witnessed those manifestations.

"Both these men are now dead, and they continued, I know, to their dying hour in the confident

belief that the work in them was of the Holy Ghost.
I mention this for the information of the reader
who may feel interested in their history, although
it is a fact which does not influence my own conviction on the subject.

"To some it may appear as if I were assuming
an importance to myself by publishing my change
of opinion, but I am in truth only clearing my
conscience, which requires me thus publicly to
withdraw a testimony which I had publicly given
when I no longer believe it myself."

The movement evidently was a revival of Montanism on a small scale. Montanism sprung up at
a crisis in the Church of the second century, when
she had to decide boldly between two courses : on
the one hand, either to hold to her old peculiarities
without adopting the accommodation theory, and
remain a sect to the end ; or, on the other hand, to
spread her network all over the world, and capture
it, but at the expense of abandoning her seriousness
and identifying herself with the secular life of the
world. Montanus, and those who took life seriously,
adopted the first course, and naturally enough fell
into many extravagances. Disdaining the favour
of emperors, they came to regard themselves as
possessing a monopoly of spiritual gifts and
graces. They anticipated the speedy end of the
world, held the same views regarding schism, and

8

practised austerities similar to those of their descendants in the west of Scotland. Official religion railed at them because they were a standing rebuke to it, and threatened its very existence. They attracted much attention, and won many converts, notably Tertullian. But the earlier movement died as well as the later one, having few elements of permanence in it. At their best, both were earnest protests against a worldly Church and an unspiritual religion. As such, they did their work well; and with all their extravagances and excrescences deserve to be remembered.

ERSKINE'S CHARACTER AND INFLUENCE

Erskine's Character worthy of his Creed—Testimonies of Dr.
Macleod Campbell and Bishop Ewing — Sympathy of
Erskine—Draws out Carlyle's best side—Example of
Magnetic Sympathy in Swiss Hotel—Did Erskine's Char-
acter render him unfit to appreciate St. Paul ?—Mr. W. E.
Gladstone's Views — Erskine tones down Calvinistic
Asperities — Life, Education — The Higher Criticism —
Testimony of F. D. Maurice.

IT is no exaggeration to say of Thomas Erskine,
that if his creed was beautiful and good, his
personal character was worthy of it, which is surely
saying a great deal. He was a most liberal-
minded thinker ; but, it has sometimes happened
that liberal-minded thinkers have been singularly
illiberal men, even as Calvinists of the high-and-
dry school have often been singularly kind-hearted,
charitable gentlemen. In other words, men may
be unworthy of their creed, or they may be
better than their creed. Erskine was the latter.
It is reported of him that he once said of his
friend Macleod Campbell : " I never saw a man

so liberal whose spirit is so solemnised." The
same fine tribute might have been applied to himself. One friend confessed that he never thought
of Erskine without thinking of God. Another,
quoting Jacob Boehme,—"The element of the bird
is the air; the element of the fish is the water;
the element of the salamander is the fire; and the
heart of God is Jacob Boehme's element," adds,—"as
I have heard Erskine quote these words I used to
think; thou art the man that Boehme describes himself to be." Bishop Ewing's tribute places Erskine
before us almost in the character of an object of
worship. "I have just come from being ten days with
Mr. Erskine in Edinburgh. It is always a great gain
to be with him. I learn more from his conversa-
tions than from all the books I read. *His looks and
life of love are better than a thousand homilies.*"

His character was open and transparent like
glass. Its dominant quality was sympathy. He
possessed a power of sympathy which seemed to
put all the people whom he met with on their best
behaviour. It was a magic wand which he only
required to wave in order to immediately command
the interest of those he spoke to, or corresponded
with, on the highest and most unutterable concerns
of life. By the working of this wondrous spell he
drew out the listener's best side, and transmuted all
he touched to gold. Who but Erskine, a master

in the art of sympathy, could have prevailed upon Thomas Carlyle to unbosom himself and lay bare the tender side of his nature ?

" It is a great evil to me," writes Carlyle, " that now I have no work, none worth calling by the name ; that I am too weak, too languid, too sad of heart, to be fit for any work, in fact, to care sufficiently for any object left me in the world to think of grappling round it and coercing it by work.   A most sorry dog-kennel it oftenest all seems to me, and wise words, if one even had them, to be only thrown away on it.   Basta-basta, I for most part say of it, and *look with longings towards the still country where at last we and our loved ones shall be together again.   Amen, amen."* [1]

" DEAR MR. ERSKINE,—I was most agreeably surprised by the sight of your handwriting again,—so kind, so welcome !   The letters are as firm and honestly distinct as ever " — (Erskine had then entered his 80th year) ;—" the mind, too, in spite of its frail *environments*, as clear, *plumb-up*, calmly expectant, as in the best days : right so : *So* be it with us all, till we quit this dim sojourn, now grown so lonely to us, and our change come !   ' Our Father which art in heaven, Hallowed be Thy name, Thy will be done ' ;—what else can we say ?   The other night,

[1] *Letters*, 481.

in my sleeplesss tossings about, which were growing
more and more miserable, these words, that brief and
grand Prayer, came strangely into my mind, with
an altogether new emphasis, as if *written* and shining
for me, mild, pure splendour, on the black bosom of
the Night there; when I, as it were, *read* them
word by word,—with a sudden check to my imperfect wanderings, with a sudden softness of composure which was much unexpected.   Not for
perhaps thirty or forty years had I once formally
repeated that Prayer;—nay, I never felt before how
intensely the voice of Man's soul it is; the inmost
aspiration of all that is high and pious in poor
Human Nature; right worthy to be recommended
with an 'After this manner pray ye.'

.   .   .   .   .   .

"I am still able to walk, though I do it on com-
pulsion merely, and without pleasure except as in
work *done*.   It is a great sorrow that *you* now get
fatigued so soon, and have not your old privilege
in this respect.   I only hope you perhaps do not
quite so indispensably need it as I; with me it is
the key to *sleep*, and, in fact, the one medicine
(often ineffectual, and now gradually oftener) that
I ever could discover for this poor clay tabernacle
of mine.   I still keep working after a weak sort,
but can now do little, often almost nothing:—all
my little 'work' is henceforth *private* (as I calculate)

—a setting of my poor house in order, which I would fain finish *in time*, and occasionally fear I shan't. Dear Mr. Erskine, good be ever with you. Were my hand *as little* shaky as it is to-day I would write to you oftener. A word *from* you will ever be welcome here."[1]

The magnetic power of his sympathy sometimes produced extraordinary effects. One of these occurred in Switzerland in the hotel where he was staying. He had just listened to a distressing tale of sorrow concerning one of the guests at the hotel, and was feeling an intense sympathy for the unfortunate man. The sufferer (who was as unknown to Erskine as Erskine was to him) at that moment entered the room, and "such was the effect of the look of sympathy that Mr. Erskine bent upon him that the sufferer threw himself into his arms, and laid his head upon his shoulders weeping." To quote Principal Shairp's words: "It was as if inside his man's understanding he had, as it were, a woman's heart." Like George Eliot, what he valued most in men was not so much the gifts and qualities that rendered them unique, the talents or the genius that marked them off from the vulgar herd, but the common qualities which they possessed "as members of one family, of

[1] *Letters*, 488.

one race, children of one Father redeemed by one
Saviour who is the common Head of all." Jean
Welsh Carlyle's faithful old nurse Braid, and her
poor bedridden son, whom Erskine often visited in
their humble home in Edinburgh, were persons
whose character was more to his liking than that
of Frederick the Great. For the same reason he
greatly enjoyed the line of the old Hebrew psalmist,
"Thou art He that took me out of my mother's
womb," because it seemed to represent Him of
whom it was written as finding rest for his spirit
not in any possession which marked him off from
other men, but in that which he held in common
with the human race.

For the same reason he had almost a craze for
showing kindness to persons whom he met by
the merest accident, whom he had never known
previously and whom he might never see again.
Persons of the type of the Sicilian, whom he
came across in the island of Ischia, were at
once spoken to and treated as brothers. On the
occasion referred to he found the poor man in a
state of illness and friendlessness, and for weeks
together he tended him and refused to leave him
because he appeared so weak and lonely. "The
secretary to the French Embassy here, a friend of
mine, tells me that he is going to-morrow to Paris
with despatches; and as a motive to give him

letters, he says that he goes quicker than the post. *I should like to go myself, but I cannot leave the poor invalid."* When strangers and foreigners in distress came in for such unusual kindness at the hands of this benevolent man, it is possible that some will wonder whether he remembered the case of those who had more claim upon him—his friends and neighbours and fellow-countrymen at home, —or whether he was a Good Samaritan of the romantic order. He was not. In 1842, during a season of distress in the country, we find him writing to his friend, Dr. Macleod Campbell:—

"I had proposed being in Glasgow before now, and even I had thought of going to Oban and seeing your dear father, and refreshing my spirit by the sight of heathery mountains which I have not looked on for many years. But man does not direct his own way, and it is neither on this mountain nor in Jerusalem that we are to worship the Father. *I have been kept at home by the feeling that at this time of general destitution all those who have any property or any capability of being helpful to their fellow-creatures, by giving them employment or otherwise, should be at their posts."* To other correspondents he writes a little later on in the same year (1842):—

"I have been surrounded for the last six months with starving unemployed labourers, and I have been giving them work to an amount varying from twenty to thirty, which, being so much above my usual expenditure, I find myself tolerably drained : and besides, the faces of those whom I have been obliged to refuse employment to, seem to me to reproach me for every shilling which I spend out of my own neighbourhood."

Nor, as we can well suppose, was it only the bodily distresses of his less fortunate brethren that Erskine delighted to heal. He respected their higher needs as well, and had oil and wine for these needs in the case of every one of them. He was a true priest. Once, as the late Dean Stanley tells us, he met a shepherd in the Highlands, to whom, "in that tone which combined in so peculiar a manner, sweetness and command," he put the unlooked-for question, "Do you know the Father?" The shepherd, taken aback, said nothing; but the wonderful tone and personality of the questioner made so deep an impression upon his mind that he could not get past the question put to him, nor yet dismiss it from his mind, with the remarkable result that, meeting Mr. Erskine many years afterwards, the shepherd recognised him at once, and said, "I know the Father now." In his personality there were combined a broad love of man as man which was modern, with the tone and authority of the Hebrew prophet which belonged to an antique past. He had a fellow-feeling for human error and infirmity, which made him the brother of his fellow-men, who at the same time felt that he belonged to another realm than theirs—

> " Where the immortal shapes
> Of bright aërial spirits live insphered
> In regions mild, of calm and serene air,
> Above the smoke and stir of this dim spot
> Which men call Earth."

To some, Erskine's character may lack the interest that is derived from moral struggle and antagonism, may seem too faultless and free from human passion,—a thing " too bright and good, for human nature's daily food." On the other hand, it is to be remembered that he had a larger share of sorrow than falls to most men, and that brought with it its own peculiar dangers and trials. If, again, he had less animal grossness to suppress within him than falls to the lot of the average man, he may have had an organism all the more acutely sensitive to the finer deflections from the moral law. Certainly, nothing could be less true than to suppose that he had little inward conflict of soul, and no repentance that did not need to be repented of. Towards the end of his life we find him making the confession, " I can look upon nothing in my whole life that I do not more or less condemn and grieve over." At the same time, he seems to have had such exceptional immunity from the ordinary infirmities of human nature, that though it could not entirely exempt him from inward struggle, or raise him above the need of humility, it may yet have produced that tendency to one-sidedness that is observable in the structure of his theological system. The moral consciousness out of which springs the full appreciation of Pauline theology, for example, was an experience of which probably he had only a slight acquaintance. I think he was one to whom Mr. Gladstone's remarkable words apply in his essay on the life of the Prince Consort.

"There are persons, though they may be rare and highly exceptional, in whom the atmosphere of purity has not been dimmed, the forces of temptation are comparatively weak, and at the same time the sense of duty is vigorous and lively. . . . Persons such as these, ever active in human duty, need not be indifferent about religion; on the contrary, they may be strongly religious. . . . They may 'give their heart to the Purifier, their will to the Will that governs the universe'; and yet they may but feebly and partially appreciate parts of Christian doctrine: nay, they may even, like Charles Lamb, the writer of these beautiful and powerful words, hold themselves apart from its central propositions. So it may come about that the comparative purity of a man's nature, the milder form of the deterioration he inherits, the fearless cheerfulness with which he seems to stand and walk in the light of God's presence, may impair his estimate of the warmer, more inward, and more deeply spiritual parts of Christianity. Further, they may altogether prevent him from appreciating the gospel on its severer side. He may generously give credit to others for dispositions corresponding with his own ; and may not fully perceive the necessity, on their behalf, of that law which is made not for the righteous, but for the ungodly and the profane, of those threatenings and prohibitions wherewith the gospel seeks to arrest reckless or depraved spirits in their headlong course, to constrain them to come in, and to rescue them as brands from the burning. In a word, he may unduly generalise the facts of his own mental and moral constitution." [1]

Turning now from a consideration of Erskine's character to an estimate of his influence, it goes without saying that that has been great, and greatest among those who have been themselves leaders of religious thought. It is not, of course, possible to determine a great teacher's influence with anything like the precision with which we can record

[1] *Gleanings*, i. 55.

the various editions of his books, but it is surely
possible to say to what extent his thoughts have
entered the mind of the age, and have become
enlisted among the ruling ideas of the world.
Applying such a high standard to his writings, it
will be allowed, I think, that his influence has
been unmistakably great.   If we single out any
one of his favourite topics in the department of
Ethics or Theology, the peculiar treatment of which
appeared so revolutionary at the period of its first
publication, it may be confidently asserted that
there are few teachers of the present day, exercising religious influence over their fellow-men,
who are not indebted to him.   His influence has
been great, and helpful even on those matters on
which, in the opinion of many, the conclusions which
Erskine reached were rash and unwarranted.

But leaving these aside for the present, take
the subject of Calvinistic teaching, as that was
popularly understood in Erskine's day.   No one
will deny that the criticism which he applied
to it was just that which was imperatively
demanded.   He was a firm believer in Calvinistic doctrine, and repeatedly acknowledged his
indebtedness to it.   It was he who pronounced
the truest eulogium that was ever passed upon it,
when he said that Arminianism was a wolf in
sheep's clothing, but Calvinism was a sheep in

wolf's clothing. Almost in the last year of his life he expressed himself as under deep obligation to the Calvinian atmosphere which he had insensibly breathed from his childhood, though he took exception to many things that were fathered upon Calvinism, and even regarded some of its propositions as " scriptural excesses." No good Calvinist has ever upheld Calvinism as an infallible system. " My Christianity," said Dr. Chalmers, " approaches nearer Calvinism than any of the isms : but broadly as Calvin announces truth, he does not bring it forward in that free and spontaneous manner which I find in the New Testament." In these true and courageous words, Chalmers went a great length for the times in which he lived and the responsible position which he filled, but, of course, it was nothing to the lengths to which Erskine in his more independent position felt himself bound to go, and in which so many subsequent teachers have followed him. Erskine attacked some things in the system as tending to obscure the Christian conception of God as well as impair and needlessly darken the destiny of man. He attacked these so effectually that sects, springing up in chivalrous response to the newer light, having leavened the whole religious community with their own large spirit, now find themselves in the ungrateful position of having their occupation gone.

With regard to another of Erskine's messages to
the world, that human life in the purpose of God
means the education of the individual man rather
than his probation, although it has to be admitted
that his advocacy of this great practical truth was
not free from the tendency to one-sidedness which
we have noticed before, it also is an instance of the
fruitful growth of the seed which he so quietly
sowed.   A statement of his ideas on this subject in
his own impressive words will suffice to show how
thoroughly we have become familiarised with them,
how fully they have entered into the mind of the
present age, and how secure a place they have
received within the domain of our religious thought
and experience.

"There are few religious phrases that have had
such a power of darkening men's minds as to their
true relation to God, as the common phrase that
we are here in a state of probation—under trial as
it were.   We are not in a state of trial : we are in
a process of education directed by that eternal
purpose of love which brought us into being.   It is
impossible to have a true confidence in God whilst
we feel ourselves in a state of trial : we must
necessarily regard him not as a Father but as a
Judge, and we must be occupied with the thought
how we are to pass our trial.   We know our own
unworthiness, and though we know that we have a

Saviour, there must still be a degree of alarm in the thought of that judgment-seat. But when we have once realised the idea that we are in a process of education which God will carry on to its fulfilment, however long it may take, we feel that the loving purpose of our Father is ever resting on us, and that the events of life are not appointed as testing us whether we will choose God's will or our own, but real lessons to train us into making the right choice. If probation is our thought, then forgiveness or receiving a favourable sentence is our object; if education is our thought, then progress in holiness is our object. If I believe myself in a state of education, every event, even death itself, becomes a manifestation of God's eternal purpose: on the probation system, Christ appears as the deliverer from a condemnation; on the education system, He appears as the deliverer from sin itself." [1]

Erskine's attitude on questions of the higher criticism would not now be considered satisfactory. I fancy it was very similar to that of Jowett, not an attitude of distrust or indifference altogether, but to some extent one of dissatisfaction and disappointment. Jowett, in a letter to Mrs. Ward, wishes that the age of biblical criticism would pass, that we might enter a larger atmosphere. He does

[1] *Letters*, 215.

not see that we have gained anything important from it, or can gain anything, even if it made plain to us the manner of the composition of the Old and New Testaments, and gave us the correct reading of every text, date, and fact connected with the Bible. It was not, according to Jowett, with the very words of Christ that we were now concerned, but with the best form of Christianity for the use of the world at the present day. "There is an ideal which we have to place before us, intimately connected with practical life—nothing if not a life— which may be conveniently spoken of as the life of Christ: and we have to adjust this, which we can feel within us, and which we see externally shown by a natural gift in a very few persons, to all the political and ecclesiastical and social forms which it takes around us."[1] Without making Erskine responsible for other men's views on the delicate matters here referred to, it may be taken as certain that neither the methods of the higher criticism nor its conclusions interested him very profoundly. It is true, the science of criticism was but in its infancy in this country in Erskine's latest years. Bishop Colenso had just come forward with his attempts at reconstructing the Pentateuch. Erskine was one of those who leaned to the conservative side. He could have wished Colenso had kept his MS.

[1] *Life of Jowett.*

unprinted for years, until the faith of the masses
was able to bear it. For himself, he was frank
enough to confess that he found no difficulty in
regard to the toleration of such views as the Bishop
was propounding. " I have myself always been
seeking for a self-evidencing light in divine truth,
not resting on any authority whatever." If
Erskine did not, and probably could not, be
expected to hail the application of literary criticism
to the Bible, this was not owing to any unscholarly
fear as to its destructiveness. He believed that
Revelation rested on a foundation that criticism
could not imperil, and did not seek to imperil.
True criticism could have no other result than
that of illuminating Revelation. " Any revelation,
whether inspired or uninspired, must owe its whole
value to its being the discovery of truth, which
remains true independently of that revelation, and
which can be profitable to us only in so far as it
produces a conviction in our minds from its own
light, unaffected by the inspiration or non-inspiration
of the revelation."

It is only possible to speculate how far Erskine's
influence would have been affected had he been a
servant of the Church that had deposed Macleod
Campbell, and that would most assuredly have
deposed him. On the one hand, a churchman's
training and responsibility might have exercised a

restraining influence upon his utterances ; he might
not have spoken out his thoughts so frankly; he
might have published less.   On the other hand, a
heresy prosecution would have made his name
better   known, and circulated   his   views   more
extensively.   However these things might have
been, Erskine's influence as a teacher of spiritual
Christianity has been great, greater than he has
ever received credit for.   It is believed, however,
that many teachers of religion are to be found in
every part of the civilised world who would readily
subscribe to the noble testimony of an English
Nonconformist minister : " I often feel my religion
so fresh and green, and my preaching so young and
joyous, that I am surprised, and, inwardly thanking
God, cannot but remember that it is to Erskine as
the instrument I owe all my light and life."   The
influence that he exerted over one great leader of
men alone—Frederick Denison Maurice—was great
enough of itself to determine Erskine's place in the
roll of the world's great lights.   Maurice, whom
Charles Kingsley described as " the most beautiful
human soul whom God has ever, in His great
mercy, allowed me, most unworthy, to meet with
upon this earth," dedicated in 1852 his *Prophets
and Kings of the Old Testament* to Erskine, and
thus acknowledged his indebtedness to him :

" The pleasure of associating my name with

yours, and the kind interest which you expressed
in some of these sermons when you heard them
preached, might not be a sufficient excuse for the
liberty which I take in dedicating them to you.
But I have a much stronger reason. I am under
obligations to you which the subject of this volume
especially brings to my mind, and which other
motives, besides personal gratitude, urge me to
acknowledge. . . . Have we a gospel for men, for
all men ?   Is it a gospel that God's will is a will to
all good, a will to deliver them from all evil ?   Is
it a gospel that He has reconciled the world unto
Himself ?   Is it this absolutely, or this with a
multitude of reservations, explanations, contradictions ?   It is more than twenty years since a book
of yours brought home to my mind the conviction
that no gospel but this can be of any use to the
world, and that the gospel of Jesus Christ is such
a one. . . . Many of my conclusions may differ
widely from those into which you have been led :
I should be grieved to make you responsible for
them.   But if I have tried in those sermons to show
that the story of the Prophets and Kings of the Old
Testament is as directly applicable to the modern
world as any Covenanter ever dreamed, but that it
is applicable because it is a continual witness for a
God of righteousness, not only against idolatry, but
against that notion of a mere sovereign, Baal or

Bel, which underlies all idolatry, all tyranny, all
immorality, I may claim you as their spiritual
progenitor."

Many years after the expulsion of Maurice from
King's College, London, he again felt constrained to
acknowledge his indebtedness to Erskine. He was
then a professor in Cambridge, and exercising a
wonderful influence over the rising generation with
his lectures on "Casuistry, Moral Theology, and
Moral Philosophy."

"I do feel very often, when I am trying to tell
the young men at Cambridge of the conscience
that is in each of them, and who is speaking to it,
how much you have taught me about that, and how
I should like to share my thoughts upon it with
you. I think I have dwelt too exclusively on the
social aspect of truth. I have been so much
startled at some prevalent denials, especially by
Bain, of individual responsibilities and freedom,
that I have gone to that and made it the starting-
point of my moral instructions."

Erskine died at Edinburgh on March 28, 1870.
During the last year or two of his life he had
two great trials, in the loss of his sisters Christian (Mrs. Stirling) and David (Mrs. Paterson)
within a few months of one another. For years
they had been his devoted companions in life. He
leaned on them both for spiritual sympathy, and for

aid in all his secular arrangements.   Erskine, at
that time on the verge of eighty, found solace in
his favourite psalms, and in the thoughts and
studies which had long delighted him.   Friends
whom he had never failed in their dark and cloudy
day now hastened with their sympathy,—Carlyle
in particular, who thus wrote in his strong yet
tender way: "It is the saddest feature of old age
that the old man has to see himself daily grow
more lonely; reduced to commune with the
inarticulate Eternities and the Loved Ones now
unresponsive who have preceded him thither.
Well, well: there is blessedness in this too, if
we take it well.   There is a grandeur in it, if
also an *extent* of sombre sadness, which is new
to one ; nor is hope quite wanting, — nor the
clear conviction that those whom *we* would most
screen from sore pain and misery are now safe
and at rest.   It lifts one to real kingship withal,
real for the first time in this scene of things.
Courage, my friend ; let us endure patiently and
act piously to the end.   Shakespeare sings pathetically somewhere—

> ' Fear no more the heat of the sun,
>   Nor the furious winter's rages ;
> *Thou* thy weary task has done,
>   Home hast gone, and ta'en thy wages ' ;

—inexpugnable and well art *thou* !   These tones go

tinkling through me, sometimes, like the pious chime of far-off church bells." [1]

The day following Erskine's death, Dr John Brown, who attended him, wrote : " Our dear sweet-hearted friend is away. He died very gently last night at a quarter to ten ; laid his pathetic weary head on the pillow like a child, and his last words were, ' Lord Jesus.' " As might have been antici-pated, the scene beheld at his deathbed was as heavenly as his life had been. His nephew, who was present, declared that if many loved him for his life, more would have loved him in his death. And thus, to quote Dr. Hanna's beautiful words, " few have ever passed away from among their fellows, of whom so large a number of those who knew him best, and were most competent to judge, would have said as they did of Mr. Erskine, that he was the best, the holiest man they ever knew—the man most human, yet most divine, with least of the stains of earth, with most of the spirit of heaven."

[1] *Letters*, 260.

SELECTIONS

NATURAL RELIGION. *The Doctrine of Election* (1837).

THE INWARD WITNESS. *The Doctrine of Election.*

THE BIBLE. *The Doctrine of Election.*

CONSCIENCE. *The Doctrine of Election.*

GOD. *The Unconditional Freeness* (1828).

CHRIST. *Doctrine of Election; The Brazen Serpent* (1831).

CHRISTIANITY. *The Internal Evidence* (1821).

FAITH. *Essay on Faith* (1825); *The Unconditional Freeness.*

THE ATONEMENT. *The Internal Evidence; Essay on Faith.*

ELECTION. *Doctrine of Election.*

THE HEART MAKES THE THEOLOGIAN. *Essay on Faith.*

A GOSPEL FOR THE LIVING. *Essay on Faith.*

A GOSPEL FOR THE DYING. *The Unconditional Freeness.*

A GOSPEL FOR THE NATURAL MAN. *Essay on Faith.*

EVIL. *The Brazen Serpent.*

PRAYER. *The Unconditional Freeness.*

VAIN RELIGION. *The Unconditional Freeness; Essay on Faith.*

HAPPINESS. *The Internal Evidence.*

HEAVEN. *The Unconditional Freeness.*

CONCLUSION. *The Unconditional Freeness.*

NATURAL RELIGION

By *natural* religion I do not mean the science of theology, or that exercise of the intellect by which we trace effects to their causes, and thus arrive at a First Cause, which we call God ; but a religion which has a *real root in our nature*, so that the doctrines of it are believed not merely, or chiefly, on any outward authority whatever, nor on any process of reasoning whatever, but on the authority of an inward consciousness,—in the same way as we believe that there is a God, and that justice is right and injustice wrong, not on any outward authority, but through an inward consciousness.

And thus it will appear that by the epithet *natural*, used in this connection, I do not mean to refer to the *source* from which the suggestion of a doctrine *first comes to us*, but to the *authority* which *finally seals it to us* ; and that I include within the description of natural religion all doctrines, though coming to us by external revelation, which meet with or awaken that inward consciousness, and are thus known by us to be true, on the authority of that consciousness.

The elements of the religion which I mean are to be found in the consciousness (by whatever means it may have been awakened)—that the voice within us which condemns unrighteousness, and approves righteousness, is the voice of a Being separate from ourselves, whose approbation or disapprobation we are continually receiving, according as we obey or disobey Him; and that this being is the God who made us and upholds us, and that He has taken up this mysterious position within us, that He may direct us in the way of righteousness, and bless us in communion with Himself; and that He will assuredly punish those who resist His gracious purpose.

This description shows that I do not oppose natural religion to supernatural,—for it assumes that all religion, in so far as it is true, must be supernatural, being the incomprehensible, though conscious meeting of the Spirit of God with the spirit of man. I do not oppose it to supernatural religion, but to *conventional religion,—that is, religion adopted on external authority, without any living consciousness within our hearts corresponding to it.*

Whilst a man is not feeling the voice in his conscience to be the voice of a Great Being, who in this way comes near to him, and desires to make

Himself known to him, but is considering it and treating it as a part of himself, like his feelings of benevolence or compassion, or regard for self-preservation, he may be acknowledging the truths of theological science or of the Bible, and he may be ordering his conduct according to the received maxims of the age or country in which he happens to live; but he has not a religion which has a living root in his heart, he has a conventional and not a natural religion. He does not yet know God at first hand.

The God of theology is a power or a principle—discerned by the intelligence through a logical process; the God of the conscience is a personal being, possessing a personal character, discerned by the conscience, as light is by the eye. Those whose knowledge of God comes through theology often dispute, as the Epicureans and others, whether there be such a thing as special providence, and whether God cares about the condition of individual men, and seeks the direction of their character and conduct; whereas those who know God through their consciences, begin with these very points as the grounds and elements of their religion, and as matters not of inference, but of consciousness.

But some one may here interrupt me, and say, " I have no consciousness of this voice within me, as you are pleased to call it, being anything else

than a part of my own nature, and especially I am
not conscious of its proceeding from a Being distinct
and separate from myself; and surely you have no
right to make your own consciousness, or your
imagined consciousness, a general standard of human
consciousness, or as indicating a general fact with
regard to the condition of men."

I answer, that there are many things even in our
physical constitution which, whilst unattended to,
are not matters of consciousness, but which become
so by being attended to. Thus the action of the
stomach and of the heart, whilst we are occupied
about other things, is not matter of consciousness
to us in general. But if we read a book on the
subject of these organs, and thus have our attention
drawn to them, we gradually grow into a consciousness of their action. But this could not be unless
there were actually within us a dormant consciousness of this action prior to any such attention.
Attention could not create that consciousness; it
only awakens it.

Now, surely we are warranted to reason analogic-
ally from this fact, that there may be a similar
dormant consciousness, with regard to many things
in our moral or spiritual constitution, which it only
requires fitting circumstances to awaken, by calling
attention to it, and that therefore we ought not to
be hasty in disclaiming for ourselves the existence

of the root of any particular consciousness within us, although we are not yet alive to it.

And, in fact, all this reasoning is in perfect agreement with the general feeling and judgment of mankind; for I conceive that I am not opposing that general feeling when I say, that I believe that there are many persons in this world who, from the circumstances of their being born and brought up in the midst of ignorance and barbarism and wickedness, and in consequence of being trained from infancy to regard self-gratification as the only rule of life, have perhaps never had a distinct consciousness of the wrongness and blame-worthiness of what is wrong, or the rightness and praise-worthiness of what is right; and who yet, if they were taken out from these darkening circumstances, and if they had the qualities of justice and injustice, of self-sacrificing love and wreckless self-gratification, presented steadily to them in contrast with each other, would feel a new consciousness on these subjects awakening within them,—a new consciousness of a living principle in their hearts taking part with that which is good, and condemning all transgression of it, either in themselves or in others.

And further, I conceive that I am still in harmony with the general sense of mankind when I ascribe such a change as this in the character of

any individual to an awakening of certain principles
which had been all along in him, though dormant,
rather than to the implanting of any new ones at
the time of the change; and also, when I maintain
that unless these hitherto dormant principles be
really awakened in him, so that he himself consciously knows and approves of what is right and
condemns what is evil, not as following the opinions
or fashions of different nations of men, or orders of
society, but as feelingly tasting and discerning their
opposite natures in his own heart,—no true moral
change, but only a conventional one, can be said to
have taken place in him.

But if it be admitted to be a true statement
that the consciousness of an approving and condemning voice within the heart may long lie
dormant, and yet afterwards prove its prior existence by awakening under the influence of circumstances which call a certain degree of attention to
it, there is nothing unreasonable in the supposition
that a further degree of attention should still
further enlarge the consciousness, so that the mind
may recognise that voice to be the voice of its
Creator—of a Being separate from itself, but seeking
oneness with it.

It seems to me that this expansion of the limits
of consciousness, from the acknowledgment of the
voice to the acknowledgment of the Speaker, marks

the true connection between morality and piety, and is in fact the answer to Plato's inquiry in his *Euthyphron* as to the relation between (ⲧⲟ ὅσιον) holiness and (ⲧⲟ δικαιον) justice or rightness. I say the expansion of the consciousness,—for I do not recognise a mere intellectual inference, that there must be a speaker because there is a voice, as true religion. Such an intellectual inference may lead to the conscious recognition of the speaker, by calling attention to Him, but until it does so it is only a part of theological science.

THE INWARD WITNESS

I BELIEVE that the objections that many feel to the doctrine of the inward witness of the Spirit arise often from a misapprehension of it. It is supposed, for example, that when a man says that he has the witness of the Spirit to any doctrine, or to the interpretation of any text, he is necessarily claiming infallibility to himself on that particular subject at least.

Now, I do not deny that many persons when they say such a thing *do indeed* claim infallibility on the subject, but I deny that a person, rightly understanding what the witness of the Spirit is, would feel himself at all entitled to claim infallibility even on a subject in which he most strongly felt the confirmation of the inward witness ; because I believe that that witness witnesses not to intellectual, but to moral and spiritual truth, and I therefore do not consider it to be a revelation to a man enabling him to solve an intellectual difficulty, such as an obscure passage of Scripture, or a disputed point of church usage or history, but to be the living sympathy and apprehension with which his heart answers to, and takes hold of, any announcement of the love or righteousness of God, and any claim which God makes on man to be conformed to His likeness, wherever he meets them, or thinks he meets them. And thus I conceive that a man of a right spiritual mind, on reading a passage in which he thinks that he perceives such an announcement, or such a claim, although his perception is founded on an entire mistake of the meaning of the passage, may yet have the true witness of God's Spirit within him, to what he feels of life to his soul in it, no less certainly than if he had been right in his intellectual apprehension of the passage.

I have met with people who conceived that this doctrine of the inward witness was completely disproved by producing two acknowledged Christians opposed to each other, and maintaining, each of them, that they had the witness of the Spirit to their view of a subject. But this is no proof against it; for it is perfectly possible that each of the contending parties may connect his view of the subject with announcements of God's nature, or of man's duty, which may be most true and most quickening to his own soul—and it is to these quickening truths that the witness alone refers.

But when I say that we are not left to lean on any outward authority for our knowledge of

God, and of His ways towards us, let no one think
that I am putting aside the Bible as an authority;
for my meaning is simply this, that although many
most important truths are set before us in the
Bible which never would have entered our hearts
had they not been thus set before us, yet that,
being thus set before us, they are then only
profitable to us, and even truly believed by us,
when they awaken within us a corresponding
form of our inward spiritual consciousness, so that
we recognise them henceforth as truths which we
ourselves know to be truths, by conscious experience,
and not merely on the outward authority of the Book.

There are many facts in our intellectual experience quite analogous to this, which might be
used to illustrate it. Thus a man may be perfectly incapable of making any advance in
mathematical science by his own original and
unassisted efforts,—and yet if Euclid be put into
his hands he may find himself quite able to follow
and appreciate the reasoning, and thus to gain a
very considerable acquaintance with the subject.
His mind in consequence is filled with a new class
of ideas, which he has acquired entirely from the
reading of this book. And yet it is not on the
authority of the book that he rests his conviction
of the truth of any of the propositions contained in
it, but on his own personal discernment of their

truth. Indeed, we could not consider him to have entered in the slightest degree into their meaning if we found him resting his belief of them on the authority of the book, or on any outward authority whatever. Nor, indeed, would we call such a belief a mathematical belief at all. And yet, had not the book presented the truths outwardly to him, the inward intellectual types might have lain for ever dormant within him.

In this case we do not feel that we detract from the importance of the book when we say that it is subordinate to the inward intellectual authority; that is, when we say that it is to be judged by that authority, and that no man can believe it rightly except by discerning its agreement with that authority within him; and that any other kind of belief is not a belief which suits the subject, because it is not a belief which discerns truth in the subject.

And in the same way, we do not detract from the importance or from the authority of the Bible when we say that then only can its authority be rightly acknowledged by us, when we discern its agreement with the testimony of the spiritual witness within us—and that its great importance consists in awakening our consciousness to the presence and the instructions of that spiritual witness.

THE BIBLE

WHEN a man has once become persuaded that the Bible is divinely inspired, he often seems to think that this persuasion lays him under an obligation no longer to try or judge of the contents of the Book by his conscience, but to submit himself to all that he reads there, and to receive it implicitly;— and thus he learns to put away his conscience, and to turn it from the use for which it was given, and also to turn the Scriptures from the use for which they were given,—and yet, notwithstanding all this, to have the semblance of obeying his conscience which commands him to honour God's word. But whilst he is in this state he is lying under a strange delusion,—for he is mistaking the conviction that he ought to be believing a thing for the actual believing of it; he is mistaking submission to the authority of God for the belief of the truth of God.

The error here arises from an ignorance of God, and of His purposes towards us,—it arises from regarding God not as a loving and righteous Father

who desires for us that we should become partakers
of His love and righteousness, by appreciating the
excellence of these qualities, and loving them and
receiving them into our hearts, but as a Sovereign
who insists on our absolute submission to His be-
hests, indifferent whether we see and sympathise
with His love and righteousness in them or not.

This is to merge the moral attributes of God in
His natural attributes of power and sovereignty,—
it is to say of God that what He does is the rule of
righteousness, instead of saying that what He does
is according to righteousness. And it has also a
tendency to lead us on to say that He is more
glorified by the manifestation of His power and
sovereignty in making the creature what He will,
whether good or bad, than by the manifestation of
the influence of an apprehension of His love and
righteousness, on the heart of the creature, which
He has made capable of discerning good from evil,
—in prevailing on it, of its own free choice, to
abandon all other expectations of good, and to take
Him and His love and His righteousness for its
whole desire and its whole portion.

But this is not the religion which Jesus Christ
taught. He did not come preaching the sovereignty
of God, but preaching His righteousness, and
declaring Him to be the Father. And moreover,
He did not come in His own name—that is, He did

not come claiming submission from men, on the
ground of His own personal and official authority—
but He came requiring them to receive His doctrine,
on the ground of its intrinsic truth, as discerned by
their own consciences.   He said, " If I speak the
truth, why do ye not believe Me ? " (John viii. 46),
thus appealing to something of God within their
own hearts which could distinguish truth from
falsehood, and which they were bound to consult
in judging of the things which He said to them.
And thus it appears,—that the authority on which
the gospel is to rest is the authority of truth
recognised and felt in the conscience, and not any
outward authority, however purporting to be of God,
—and that those who do rest it on an outward
authority are really subverting its principles by
so doing.

I do not mean that a man is to sit down to the
Bible in the spirit of a judge rather than of a
disciple, but I mean that the true discipleship
consists not in a blind submission to authority, but
in the discernment and love of the truth,—not in
subjecting the conscience to a revelation which it
does not understand, but in educating and feeding
the conscience by the truth apprehended in the
revelation.

But if men were called on by Jesus to try what
He Himself personally taught them, by a light

within them we are surely bound to try by the same light the things which have come down to us through the written word. And those who would teach the things which are contained in the written word ought to remember that their teaching is really of no use unless they make them clear to the consciences of the learners,—that is, unless they show, in the things taught, a righteousness of God which the consciences of the learners can apprehend and approve.

It must be evident to every one that the sole ground on which men can be considered culpable in preferring wrong to right is the assumption that they have something within them by which they can distinguish right from wrong, and discern the excellence of what is right and the evil of what is wrong. But we all naturally and necessarily make this assumption, and consider those to be culpable who, in any circumstances, prefer wrong to right. Now *truth* in morals and in religion is only another name for what is *right*, and *falsehood* another name for what is *wrong*,—and thus that inward witness which judges of right and wrong within us is the only real test by which we can judge of truth and falsehood in religion.

That this inward witness is hardly perceptible in the case of some persons, and that its judgment is limited to outward actions in the case of others, is no objection to the statement here made. For the witness is as a seed sown in the heart of man, and if it is unused it lies dormant. But still it remains true, that it is only by the awakening and the strengthening of this witness that there is any real growth within us, either in morals or religion,— and therefore the only real instruction in the Scriptures or the doctrines of religion is that which is addressed to this witness, and which thus has a tendency to awaken and exercise it, for thus only is it possible that the Scriptures can be made " profitable for instruction in righteousness."

If therefore a teacher thinks that he is claiming honour for God's authority when he refuses to listen to the objections which a learner makes to any view of a doctrine, on the ground of conscience, and when he silences all such objections by a mere reference to the written word, he is deceiving himself ; for that which is the true authority of God, in relation to every man, is the man's own perception of righteousness,—and the teacher is only then truly claiming honour for God when he brings the doctrines to meet that perception.

I am not arguing for the right of private judgment,—I am arguing for the right of conscience, that is, *for the right which my conscience has over me.* I am not arguing for my right to say to another man, my judgment is as good as yours, but I am arguing that neither he nor I can have a right to think that we are honouring God by our faith whilst our conscience is not going along with the thing believed.

When I meet with anything in the Bible to which my conscience does not consent, I feel persuaded that I don't understand the meaning of it,—for my confidence that it comes from God assures me that if I understood it aright I should perceive its righteousness. Whilst I remain in this condition, however, I am conscious that I am not believing the thing, "for with the heart man believeth unto righteousness"; and I am certain that I cannot believe anything truly unto righteousness unless I perceive righteousness in it,—I am therefore conscious that I am *not believing* in it, and that I am *only bowing* to it. But I do not willingly rest in this condition. I examine the passages on which the doctrine in question rests,—I consider whether the meaning which I have been attributing to them is the true meaning,—I consult translations and commentaries, not with the view of taking any of them as a guide, but that I may see whether I can find in any of them an interpretation which will at the same time satisfy my conscience, and agree with the language, and harmonise with the tenor of the discourse.

CONSCIENCE

THE gospel of Jesus Christ is admirably suited to our consciences, for it teaches us principles, and deals little with particular or definite directions. It contains centres and not circumferences; it sows seeds without defining the exact form of the tree; and thus it does not relieve us from the continual necessity of the true personal teaching of God, but only ministers to it.

I am sure that there are many who, in the uncertainty and perplexity of their minds as to the steps which they ought to take, have often wished for such an oracle, either inward or outward, as I have been describing, not considering that by such a wish they have really been seeking to escape from the true teaching of God, who would have them learn themselves to judge between good and evil. I believe that this very wish to escape from uncertainty at once by a definite direction, instead of seeking to rise out of it by a patient waiting on the light in our consciences, has been the parent of Popery and of all similar religious forms.

A person by becoming a Papist relieves himself from the personal obligation of apprehending truth in the light of his own conscience, and substitutes implicit obedience in its place.

The Protestant does the same thing with regard to the *doctrines* of religion that the Papist does with regard to religion throughout. He relieves himself from the personal obligation of apprehending their truth in the light of his own conscience ; he looks to the *Bible* as the Papist looks to the *Church*, and he adopts whatever doctrines he thinks that he finds *there*, without feeling the obligation of personally seeing their truth in the light of his own conscience before he is really entitled to call himself a believer of them. He thus substitutes outward authority in the place of the light which is Life, although he condemns the Papist for doing that very thing.

There is a very interesting story, in some part of Raynal's *History of the East and West Indies*, if I remember right, which I have often reflected on in connexion with this subject. The purport of the story is,—that two missionaries, one a Christian, the other a Mussulman, arrived about the same time at an island of the Indian Ocean, and propounded their respective doctrines to the natives, who received them both with great respect and attention. After they had taken their departure the king called the people together, and said to them, that as neither he nor they were capable of deciding which of these two religions was the true one, he wished them to join with him in desiring from God that He would deliver them from their perplexity, by so ordering circumstances that the first ship which reached the island should be to them a sign, indicating that the religion of the people to whom it belonged was the true religion. He accordingly, along with his people, made this prayer; and soon after a Mahometan vessel arrived, on which the whole island became Mahometan, in obedience, as they thought, to the will of God expressed by this sign.

I can scarcely believe that the story is true, but, supposing it is true, it deserves to be considered whether the way which these people took of getting rid of their difficulty was a right way or not. To me it appears that it was decidedly a wrong way, being nothing less than a culpable renunciation of their standing as moral beings. They had that within them by which they were able, and therefore were bound, to have tried and compared the two religions; and they had no right to escape from this duty. God had set the duty before them as an opportunity of receiving a blessing through it. But the great blessing which is derived from a true religion comes through appreciating and receiving the righteousness of God which is revealed in it; and therefore they, by refusing to try it by their consciences, did in fact put from them the blessing intended. And God answered this conduct by sending the Mahometan vessel first, as if to teach us who hear of it that Mahometanism and Christianity are of equal value to those who judge of moral truth by outward authority.

I cannot help associating in my own mind this little story with that most beautiful of all stories, which Herodotus tells of a nation which had received under their hospitality, and pledged their faith to, a prince who had been driven from his dominions by Crœsus, then in the midst of his conquests. While Crœsus, with his army, was at a distance from them, they maintained their fidelity to their guest; but when he approached their boundaries, and threatened them with the weight of his vengeance if they did not deliver up his enemy, they began to hesitate, and sought counsel of an oracle whether they should give him up or not. We feel at once that they had already committed a great crime by asking counsel from an outward authority in a case which they themselves ought to have determined by consulting the authority within their own consciences; and that they deserved, as the punishment of their offence, the permission which they received to break their oaths and surrender their guest; but we hesitate, perhaps, about allowing ourselves to look on our Indian islanders as in circumstances at all similar. There is, however, a resemblance between the two cases in principle, although the degrees of culpability are certainly very different. And if my reader does not see a resemblance between them, he certainly is not yet acquainted with a living religion in his own heart,—nor does he yet see a satisfying reason why any one religion should be preferred to any other.

"The Jews seek after a sign, and the Greeks seek after wisdom, but we preach Christ who was crucified, to the Jews a stumbling-block, and to the Greeks foolishness: but to them who are called, both Jews and Greeks, Christ the power of God, and the wisdom of God." The Jews were continually asking a sign that they might be delivered from the necessity of judging doctrines by the light of God in their consciences. And the Greeks, the learned, in like manner desired to escape from conscience, and to be allowed to rest their religion on the authority of an intellectual demonstration. But the Apostle preached redemption from sin and death, through a dying to the flesh, consented to, in filial dependence on the fatherly love of God, declaring, at the same time, that his doctrine could have no other effectual witness or proper basis, but the light of God in the conscience,—the true witness of the Spirit.

The instruction indeed may, and does, come from *without*, both in morals and in religion, but that authority which seals it is *within*,—the inward spiritual consciousness which constitutes *the life* in religion as well as in morality.

This is the true natural, and, at the same time, supernatural religion to which all outward revelation must be subordinate. It is natural because God has planted it in, and suited it to, man's nature; and it is supernatural because it is the union of the nature of God with the nature of man. And the outward revelation is subordinate to it, not in the sense of being inferior to it as a manifestation of God's will, but in the sense of being a letter and not a spirit, and of being both judged by it and ultimately intended for its use, that is, for its awakening and nourishment.

In this matter there is a danger which is often fallen into, and which therefore should be mentioned—namely, that men are prone to act on the supposition that the voice in their conscience is a faculty of their own nature, like their feelings of benevolence or compassion, as when the Jews said of Jesus, "Is not this the Carpenter's son?"—and then, even although they follow it, they are not brought by it into a sense of their dependence on a

11

divine authority, which is their true creaturely
condition ; and they are not led to seek acquaintance with the speaker, because they attribute it to
themselves—and thus they do not understand the
honour, and thus lose the blessing, even when there
is a certain semblance of faithfulness to the voice.
But it is only a semblance, for every one may know
that the voice in his conscience is of a different
order from the faculties or feelings of his own
mind, *because* he knows that, however weakly it
sounds, he is sinning unless he humbles before
it the highest and strongest movements of his
spirit.

There is another evil which is fallen into by
those who do, in a certain way, acknowledge the
oneness of God with the voice in conscience.   I
mean the evil of stopping short at conscience as if
that were all, and thus losing God in conscience,
instead of finding Him in it ; their error lies in so
identifying Him with this voice in conscience as to
bring Him down to the level of a mere voice, or
intimation of right and wrong, instead of rising up
through the voice to an acquaintance with Himself
from whom the voice comes, and who sends it forth
for the express purpose of leading man up to Himself.   Conscience is the link between flesh and
spirit,—it is an *entrance* by which the voice of the
Word of God enters into man, calling for the sub-

mission of his heart and will, and through which
He would communicate Himself personally and
consciously, if man would submit his heart and
will and seek His manifestation. And because the
voice is the voice of the living Word, therefore
it not only gives direction as to what ought to be
done, but it is also, in those who yield to it, an
efficient worker, working in them not to will only,
but to do of His good pleasure. And thus it is
that the apostle applies even to the unbelieving
Jews the words which Moses addressed to their
fathers: "Say not in thine heart who shall ascend
up into heaven to bring Christ down, or who shall
descend into the deep to bring Christ up; for the
word is nigh thee, in thy mouth and in thy heart,
that is, the word of faith which we preach,"—that
Jesus whom we preach outwardly is *the same Word*
who is nigh unto every man in his mouth and in his
heart.

The Bible is given to us to teach us who it is
that is speaking in our hearts, that we may be
persuaded to seek acquaintance with Him and to
take hold of His strength that we may be delivered
from the voice and power of the evil spirit working
in our flesh, and may be lifted out of sin, and
misery, and death. It is given us to make us
acquainted with God in our own flesh, who stands
knocking at every heart. Jesus is not merely a

character or personage in a book; He is a real substantial being whom we have not to seek for at a distance, nor strive to picture to ourselves by an effort of the imagination. It is He who, however hitherto unknown or misnamed by us, is now in our own hearts condemning evil and reproaching us for yielding to it, and holding out to us a fearful looking for of judgment if we continue in it. Let us listen to Him; He hath come in the name of the Lord to bless us by turning us away from our iniquities.

The Bible tells us of things which are true in our own hearts; it does not make them true. It is in this respect like a book on anatomy, which describes the various organs of our system, as the heart and the liver, etc., but it cannot make them nor give them if they are awanting. So the Bible can tell me that the power which condemns sin within me is the living Word of God in my mouth and in my heart, but it does not put it there. It may tell me that *I have* a Saviour, but it does not *make* a Saviour. It may tell me that what I have long known in my own heart under another character, under a false and mistaken character as a taskmaster and rebuker only, is really my Saviour and my God; but if there were no such rebuker really in me, this information would be of no use to me.

Persons professing Christianity often speak of the natural conscience, as they call it, disrespectfully, and yet all the true Christianity that ever finds a place in man's heart must enter through that door. *That* is the point of connection between God and man, the place of meeting,—there it is where man either receives God or rejects Him. What they mean to condemn is the misjudgment which a man, whilst he still lives in the flesh, forms of what the voice speaks within him. The light shineth in the darkness, but the darkness comprehendeth it not. Whilst the man is living in the purpose to keep his own way and will, he is living in the darkness, and cannot truly comprehend even what he sees of the light ; but when he truly desires to be directed by that condemning light within him, then he comes into the light, and will be enabled more and more to comprehend it. This is the retribution which is continually going on in man's life, and its equity rests on the fact of his really possessing a capacity to take part with, and yield himself either to the Spirit of God or to the spirit of darkness.

Theologians say well when they say that man by the Fall lost all power of doing good ; but surely they say not well when they do not acknowledge that through the Redemption this power has been restored with advantage. For what else can be the meaning of these words, "Where sin abounded, there hath grace much more abounded." And I appeal to every candid reader of the Bible, whether he does not feel that these words might be rightly taken as the sample and text and epigraph of the whole book. There is a spiritual seed given through Jesus to every man at the commencement of his life that he may trade with it; and according to his faithfulness or unfaithfulness in using it, so is his capacity for receiving a further blessing. He may at any time turn from his unfaithfulness, and then he is capable of a further blessing; but whilst he refuses to hear the voice, he is necessarily rejecting all blessings.

GOD

I HAVE sometimes been led to think that in our modern systems of religion the relation between the Creator and the creature is too little regarded, and too much merged in the particular doctrines of Christianity. No doubt it may be answered, that this relation is supposed and taken for granted in all religions,—but this is not enough. The creative and sovereign and personal omnipotence of God is, to our minds, the subjective basis of deity; and the sentiment of creaturely dependence on Him, which rises out of it and corresponds to it, is the basis of religion in the creature. All the doctrines of Christianity are but the expressions of the character of the omnipotent Creator. They are His modes of acting, but He himself is the great thing. Without the sense of His living reality, and the sentiment of relation to Him, there is no religion, and Christianity becomes a mere set of notions. There can be no doubt that a great deal of the Christianity of the world is of this spurious kind, or at least has a mixture of it. And there

are times in which God, by His dealings with us,
sends a fearful conviction of it into the heart.   He
brings a genuine reality, such as death, and sets it
before us, and makes us feel how mere notions
melt into nothing at its˙ presence, and that no
religion is of any value which does not unite us to
God by a bond as real as death is real.   The
living personality of God, if I may use the expression, must animate and fill out the Christian
doctrines,—otherwise they only tend to add a fatal
security to the sleep of the soul.   They may be
subjects of talk to us, as the gods of gold and silver
furnished talk to Belshazzar and his lords, until some
providence surprise us, as the handwriting on the
wall surprised them, and make us feel and know
what it is to be in the presence of the real God
whom we have not glorified.

I feel persuaded that no idea of a power external
to us, however great, can ever produce the sentiment of creaturely dependence on the heart,—there
must be the sense of God within us, as the root
and basis of our being, as the continual supplier of
strength for thought and action, and the fountain
from the which our current runs, or else dries up.
The Bible is full of this feeling of God, subjective
as well as objective.   He is there not only the
light which the eye sees, but He is the power of the
eye to see the light.

It is a truth which ought to produce much watchfulness and self-distrust, that practical atheism may enter into the confession of religion, and may even become a zealous partisan of orthodox Christianity. It is the God who is revealed and contained in the doctrines that alarms and assails the independence of the natural man. When they are separated from Him and His omnipotence, when they become mere syllogisms or emblazonments, they can take their place under the dark shadow of the atheism of the heart as well as the syllogisms or emblazonments of any other science. How different are these *forms* from the overawing reality with which the doctrines are animated in the Bible. And oh, how different is the effect produced by them on the hearts of their partisans,— from those cries and breathings of the creature after the Creator, which was embalmed in the sacred record, and which still seem to ascend to heaven like incense from an altar. " Thy hands have made me, and fashioned me, give me understanding, that I may keep Thy commandments." " I will abide in Thy tabernacle for ever, I will trust in the covert of Thy wings." " I am Thine, oh save me." Happy spirit, thou hast found thy fountain, thy cry enters with acceptance into the ears of the Lord of Sabaoth. " When thou saidst unto me, Seek My face, my heart said unto Thee,

Thy face, Lord, will I seek." Surely this sweet communion between heaven and earth is true religion. Oh for the putting forth of that power which made the deaf to hear, and the dumb to speak, that such sounds might enter our hearts and draw forth such answers. To a spirit thus bound by a real bond to the real God, life and death are equal, for it finds the will of God in either, and His will is its delight. It finds God in everything, and God is its portion. When Jesus says, "Behold, I come quickly," it answers, "Even so, come, Lord Jesus." This is to walk with God.

It is a question which I have often heard asked, —"Do you think that the belief of such or such a doctrine, or of such or such a view of a doctrine, is essential to salvation?" This question always seems to me to indicate a mistake in the mind of the asker as to the nature of salvation. The heart which truly loves God as its good and its portion has got salvation; for salvation is the love of the heart for God. Any belief which produces this love is consistent with salvation; and any belief which does not and cannot produce this love is inconsistent with salvation. But let no one mistake. It is quite possible to love a God who, after all, may not be the true God, but a mere idol of the imagination. God has told us Himself in His word what He is, and what He has done, so that we

may know Him and love Him in His true character.
If we love God for something that He is not,—as,
for example, for a good-natured indifference whether
His creatures are holy or not,—we do not love God,
but a lie. A true knowledge of God is necessary
to a true love of God, as it is only a true love of
God which can produce conformity to the true will
of God in the heart of the creature. The evil,
then, of taking up a wrong doctrine, or a wrong
view of a doctrine, does not lie in this—that God
punishes a man for not believing one thing more
than another; but in this—that it interferes with
the great purpose of religion, namely, that the love
of God, and the Christ of God, may abide in the
heart of man, conforming his mind and will to the
mind and will of God.

All are pardoned, but believers are a little flock.
Why is this? This is the great mystery in religion.
Here we pass into the infinite, and are lost. One
is taken, and another left. One heart is made to
hear the voice of God, and learns from that teaching
voice what flesh and blood cannot reveal,—another
reads the Bible, and hears sermons, and goes through
the forms of prayer, and seems even to long after
spiritual religion; and yet he continues a stranger
to spiritual communion with God. What is the
meaning of this? God is the Great King in all
the earth.—He doth what seemeth Him good. But

He has promised the Holy Spirit to them that ask
Him.   And yet the very disposition to ask them is
His own gift.   But the language of the Bible, in
inviting sinners to God, is so free that we must
either suppose that there is a deception in the
Bible, or we must suppose that every man has the
power of coming to God if he chooses.   Let us bow
before Him whose thoughts, although above our
thoughts, and whose ways, although above our
ways, are yet thoughts and ways of everlasting love
towards our fallen race.   We are of yesterday and
know nothing.   Let us look unto Him, and He will
save us.   The way is open.

CHRIST

GOD in our nature—that is, Christ—is the root of the new sap or eternal life in man, without which no man could have been righteous, and by the presence of which in our nature every man may be righteous. This is the root which connects the whole tree of man with God and heaven, as the carnal Adam is the root which connects it with Satan and corruption;—for the tree has two roots and two saps, and the atonement is just that acting of Christ, the new root, that voluntary dying, or shedding out by Him of the old sap, or corrupt will of man,—through which He separated Himself and all the branches that would adhere to Him, altogether and for ever, from the corruption and condemnation which belonged to, and lay upon, that old sap,—that so they might be filled exclusively with the holy sap, the eternal life, and bear the eternal blessing which rests upon it. But the adherence which the branch gives to Him, which is the righteousness of faith, is just a repetition of the same acting, by which He, the root,

173

separated Himself acceptably to God—namely, a voluntary dying or shedding out of the old sap, performed by the branch, in the power of the new sap communicated to it from the root, and without which it would be incapable of performing it.

This view of these doctrines connects them distinctly with the conscience. We must acknowledge that that corrupt sap or life within us, which seeks self-gratification instead of righteousness, is indeed the source of all the evils of our condition, and deserves the punishment of sorrow and death which God has laid upon it—and we must also acknowledge that the only way of escaping from the bondage of that corrupt life is by getting quit of it, or by shedding it out; but this we could not do without another principle of life within us, in the strength of which we might do it, and yet survive. To bring this principle of life, the eternal life, into the whole race, so as to be within the reach of every man, was the work of the root, and He effected it by shedding out the life which belongs to the flesh and blood, in which He along with the other children of the family partook; and to receive this principle of life, thus brought within their reach, so that it should become their own life, is that co-operation which is required of all men, and in which their trial consists, and which they can only effect by consenting in like manner to the shedding out of the corrupt life of the flesh, in the strength of the new principle.

The root does important things for the tree, but in doing them it is not a substitute for the tree,— nor is its action intended to dispense with the co-operating action of the branches. It commences a process which they are to carry on in the power communicated to them through it. They could not have commenced the process, but the root by commencing it has put it in their power to carry it on.

Our Great Root received the sap for us, in saying, "Not My will, but Thine be done"; that is, by dying to the will of the flesh, and consenting to the punishment laid on the flesh,—and we can receive it from Him to be our life only by following out the same process. And thus the history of Christ is not only the history of God's love in calling us to be partakers of His nature and blessedness, but is also a model of the way in which alone we can truly receive the unspeakable gift.

Before the Fall, God and man were united by the law of love. This was the bond—this was the medium of communion, and the bond was both of God and of man, because love is God's nature, and whilst man continued faithful it was his nature. And through this medium God communicated and man received all blessings, and all these blessings were but different forms of love. But when man fell this bond of love was broken, and there was no longer a medium of communion between God and man. Then it was that God promised the seed of the woman who was to destroy the works of the devil : that is, who was to renew the broken bond, and restore the interrupted communion by becoming Himself the medium or mediator of communion—Himself, who was the *living law of love*. And thus He did it. He was Himself Jehovah, and He assumed to Himself the nature which had fallen, and thus within His own person He united the two natures. On the one side He was one with the Godhead, on the other side He was one with the fallen manhood.

This was the plan of that living bond by which man was to be again united to God, and to be put in a condition of receiving out of His fulness. But this bond had to be made perfect through sufferings. " It became Him for whom are all things, and by whom are all things, in bringing many sons to glory, to make the Captain of their salvation perfect through sufferings." And why through sufferings ? What pleasure could the Father take ni the sufferings of His holy child Jesus ? for it is written that He did take pleasure in them. It *pleased* the Lord to bruise Him. Now, compare this with that other word, "I have no pleasure in the death of (the wicked) him that dieth, saith the Lord." Reader, do you understand the agreement of these two passages? God has no pleasure in the mere suffering of any creature, even although that suffering be the merited infliction of a righteous law, much less in the sufferings of a righteous person. If God had pleasure in the execution of a just sentence, He would have pleasure in the death of the wicked; but He says that He has none. It is not then in suffering, as suffering, or as the execution of a sentence, that God takes pleasure. It is not because the Godhead of Jesus gave a character of infinity to His sufferings, so as to make them infinitely exceed in weight the deserved sufferings of all the individuals of the human race, that God takes pleasure in them; for if God has no pleasure in the merited punishment of one sinner, He can have no pleasure in the punishment of millions. The Father's pleasure in the sufferings of Jesus then did not arise from their being a just satisfaction to the law, *in the sense of their meeting the law in its demand of so much punishment to answer so much sin.* Wherein then did their value consist in the Father's eyes?

There was something in the character of those

12

sufferings which glorified God, with the incommunicable glory which is due to Him, on the ground of which it became Him righteously to surround the sinful fallen race, of which He had become the head, with the light of His reconciled countenance.

In the first place, there was infinite glory given to Jehovah, by the coming forth of the Word, the second person in the Godhead, to declare the character of the Godhead. When we consider what love is, and that God is love, and that the glory of God is love, and that there is no love but of God, we see that none could rightly and fully declare this glory except God Himself, and that therefore there is an exceeding excellence and fitness in the manifestation of the Godhead by the Word made flesh, and that the complacency of the Father in this work of the Son must be infinite.

The Father's heart was yearning over the works of His hands that had destroyed themselves just by disbelieving in His love. The calumny had been uttered against Him by the devil, that He did not love man, that He grudged man a happiness, and man had believed it and was ruined by the belief of it. Now, how was this to be answered? God was the Omnipotent God, and He might have sat on the throne of heaven, and

commanded things to be as He would have them.
But omnipotence is not love, and love alone
could answer this devil's lie. Therefore the Son
answered it in love. This was a thing, let me say
it with deepest reverence, that God could not do
by a messenger or a proxy. And therefore it was
Jehovah Himself that did it. God loved every
man, even in the loathsomeness of his pollution,
even in his state of bitterest enmity, with a love
that made Him willing to taste death for every
man. This love was to be declared to answer the
devil's calumny. But how was it to be declared?
God might have sent a messenger who would have
been highly honoured by the commission of declaring His love to the guilty, and by suffering
death in the execution of His commission, but this
would *not* have declared *God's* willingness to die
for every man. This love could not have been
declared except by a personal sacrifice on the part
of God. It could not have been declared except
by God actually becoming man and dying for
every man. It could not avail itself of omnipotence, and God's love did not draw back from
the proof. Jesus was God, and He declared this
love by descending and condescending into the
human nature, and in that nature tasting death
for every man. The Father's love rejoiced in its
full manifestation. He was well pleased in the

only begotten Son. He saw His own perfect image, and He saw it in that very nature which had revolted—He saw it, and was well pleased. Thus only could God's love have been truly declared.

The world has various imaginations about God's love, but in this act the true love is declared. Some think that it is mere approbation, so that those only can be loved who deserve it. And some think that it is connivance, under the shelter of which they may sin without danger. Whilst others, more versed in the divine character, think it a holy benevolence, in the spirit of which God grieves over sin, and desires the righteousness and happiness of men, and would find His own full satisfaction in seeing them thus restored. But this is not love. God is all this,—He is holy, and He desires the holiness of His creatures. But He is something more than this. God is love, and love desires to be loved ; love demands fellowship, a communion of happiness, and can be satisfied with nothing short of it.

A holy benevolence could have been declared through a proxy, *love* could not. God has a personal tender affection for every man, so that He desires union and fellowship with every man. Now the Son declared this love of the Father, by coming into the *root* of the nature, that part which

Adam occupied, and thus coming into every man,
and thus testifying to the Father's loving desire
of union with every man, and thus fulfilling that
word, "I have drawn thee with cords of a man
and with bands of love." Being as the head and
root of the race, He is in every man as the root of
a tree is by its fibres, in every branch and twig
that grows from it. The fibre of that root in
every man is the cord of a man and the band of
love, wherewith God draws him. This is the
meaning of Christ being called "the second Adam."
And this is the meaning of the word also, "the
head of every man is Christ." And this is that
gospel which Paul was commissioned to preach
amongst the Gentiles, "Christ in you (yea in every
man), the hope of glory."[1] This, he tells us, is
the gospel which was preached *to every creature*
under heaven, or in the whole creation under
heaven. This must then be the true description
of God's unspeakable gift to every creature, of His
gift actually bestowed upon each one individual.
For it never could be gospel or good news to one
man to tell him that Christ was in another man
or in another class of men. It never could have
been good news to other Gentiles to have told
them that Christ was in the Colossian converts.
This could not have done them any good. No—

[1] 1 Cor. xi. 3, xv.; Rom. v.; Col. i. 27.

it was a message to themselves that Paul brought
them—a message to each man—a Christ to each
man—a Christ in each man, the hope of glory.
Behold the riches of the glory of the gospel of
Jesus—of that mystery which had been hid by
the counsel of God from ages and from generations,
before the manifestation of God in the flesh, and
which since that manifestation has been much hid
by unbelief, but which nevertheless remains true,
the great truth, the mighty secret, proclaimed from
the house-tops, and yet a secret.

But, reader, you start at this as if it were rather
to be desired or wondered at, than to be believed
as an actual fact.   Yet only consider, we are
assured, in the fifth chapter of the Romans and
fifteenth of 1st Corinthians, that Jesus Christ came
into Adam's place—actually into that place which
Adam held in relation to us—into the root of the
nature—well—is Adam in you or not?   Yes,
most assuredly he is.   Adam is in every man, just
because every man is a mere unfolding of Adam,
as the branch of a tree is a mere unfolding of the
seed out of which the tree sprung.   Adam is in
you.   Well Christ is in you also, for He came into
Adam's place.   And as the condemnation which
came by Adam, even sorrow and death, is upon
you—so also is the blessing which came by Christ
upon you, even the favour of God and the non-

imputation of sin, which, if believed, are life eternal.

But perhaps you will say, if a man does not hope in Christ, how can Christ be in him as the hope of glory? But this is a common use of the word Hope. God is called the hope of Israel even when Israel did not hope in Him, and the hope of all the ends of the earth, although they had never heard of Him. The hope of glory means the future glorious deliverer. If you see a child of remarkable promise in a decayed family, although the rest of the family do not appreciate him, you will say of him—there is the hope of the family. He is a reason of hope, though they do not see it. Even so Christ is in our decayed fallen family the hope of glory, though little appreciated, and He is in each one of the family, though unknown and unnoticed. Yes, reader, Christ is in you, the hope of glory, and you shall be presented holy and unblamable and unreprovable in the sight of the Father, if you continue in this *faith*, grounded and settled, and be not moved away from this *hope* of the gospel which ye have heard.

This is the gospel. This is that provision in the strength of which we are called on to be holy as God is holy, to be perfect in love as God is perfect, to be habitations of God through the

Spirit. Consider this call, this commandment of God, and think whether it could be possible to answer it on any lower provision than this, "Christ in you the hope of glory." We are called on to have the same mind in us as was in Christ Jesus, and yet the Spirit witnesses of the carnal mind, which is the natural mind of every man, that it is enmity against God. Now God's service is a reasonable service. Yet how is this reasonable? How is it reasonable to ask love from enmity? The reasonableness of the call lies in this, "Christ in us the hope of glory." And the Scripture tells us that we have all things that pertain unto life and godliness, in the knowledge of Him who hath called us to glory and virtue. It is in the knowledge then of Jesus Himself *in us* that we have the mind of Jesus, which is life and godliness, and glory and virtue.

The preaching then of "Christ in you the hope of glory" is just the preaching of that *first* bond by which all men are united to Christ, namely, the bond of the flesh. It is preaching God tabernacled in the flesh of every man. For what is true of the whole race is true of every individual in the race. Each man is a microcosm, a miniature of the world and of the race, and therefore when we hear of Christ coming into the flesh of our race, we in fact hear of His coming into the flesh of every man. When we hear of God *so* loving the world, we hear of His *so* loving each man of the world. It is just the root of the vine being in every one of its branches, in virtue of its fibres pervading all the branches, the withered as well as the living. Remember, Christ came into Adam's place. This is the real substitution.

It must strike every reader of the gospel history that in all His instructions Jesus constantly and directly appeals to the consciences of men, for the truth and the righteousness of what He says. He does not require any of His words to be received on His personal authority, but on the authority of their own self-evident truth. This is plainly what He means when He says that "He had not come in His own name," and that He did not speak in His own name, "but in His Father's." This also is the meaning of that word in Luke xii. 57, "Why even of yourselves, judge ye not what is right?" in which He evidently condemns the Jews for not knowing God's truth when they heard it; and it is also the meaning of that other word, "And if I say the truth, why do you not believe Me? He that is of God heareth God's words: ye therefore hear them not, because ye are not of God" (John viii. 46, 47.) He spoke the same thing outwardly which the Spirit of the Father was speaking inwardly in all consciences; and so the word was not His, but the Father's who had sent Him.

And thus He appeared in the world as the true witness of God, and as the living conscience of the whole world, giving free and willing utterance to those truths which, though suppressed and darkened and perverted in the individual consciences of men by unfaithfulness and the power of the flesh in them, yet never can be heard without calling forth a testimony that they are of God.

But it will be said that all this relates only to religious *precepts*, and that although it be granted that there are within us types corresponding to the truths which Jesus taught, it does not follow that there are any such corresponding types to the events of His history, His miraculous birth, His sacrificial death, and His resurrection, which yet constitute the chief doctrines of the Christian faith.

But if it be true that Jesus did appear indeed as the living conscience of the whole world, then in the inward history of our own individual consciences we must have the types corresponding to His outward history.

And surely it is with the purpose of leading us to look for and to find such corresponding types within us that John begins his Gospel by identifying Jesus, *first*, with God, "The Word was God"; and *then* with the Spirit or light in man's con-

science, "In Him was life; and the life was the
light of men. That was the true Light, which
lighteth every man."

For in these words the evangelist, as it were,
puts his hand on each man's heart and says to him,
"The history which you are now to read is the
history of God manifest in your flesh; but it is also
the history of this mysterious power which you feel
within your own heart,—for they are one,—and you
can only understand the outward history by compar-
ing it with your own consciousness of the inward
power. The power in you is a stream from a
Fountain; and as you cannot know the Fountain
except through the stream which has visited your
own soul, so you cannot understand the stream
except by knowing what the Fountain is from
which it flows."

And thus the reason that Jesus has a witness to
what He says in every conscience is that in every
conscience there flows a stream of spirit, of which
He is Himself the Fountain, and every utterance
of the Fountain is felt electrically through the
streams. And the reason that His actions in the
outward world have corresponding living types
within each man's conscience is—that He Himself
is truly in each man's conscience, present by His
Spirit, and seeking to manifest there, in the secret
of each man's personal consciousness, the same great

things which He outwardly and publicly manifested in His own personal humanity in the world. Seeking, I say, to manifest the same great things—and to this end inviting the willing co-operation of each individual soul, as the necessary condition, without which He cannot accomplish that inward work.

If we found a man who was resting his belief of the existence of the sun, and of its relation to our earth, merely on a book of astronomy, we should infer that he did not know what the sun was; because we should feel that if he really knew that the bright luminary which he was accustomed to see every day was the very same sun of which his book spoke, his belief of its existence would rather rest on his own personal experience of it, than on any extraneous record whatever. His book of astronomy is written with a reference to things and to facts which are open to his observation and experience; and it is impossible for him to understand the purpose of the book unless he connects with it the results of his observation and experience.

It would be a curious and eccentric phenomenon to see a man well versed in theoretical astronomy and natural history, who yet walked forth into the world and viewed the various objects in the heavens above and in the earth beneath, without ever recognising them as the same objects of which his books treated, and with the laws of which he was so well acquainted through the means of his books. Such a man would evidently have two worlds, perfectly unconnected,—the one, the world of his experience; the other, the world of his theory; and in consequence of this separation his theory would be without the life of experience, and his experience would be without the light of theory.

There is surely something very like this presented to us continually in the case of that great multitude of religious people who separate their religious knowledge received through revelation from their own personal consciousness of spiritual things, which I have here called natural religion. Whilst a man's belief of the being and character of Jesus Christ rests *solely* on revelation, it is manifest that he has never yet in his own mind connected or identified the idea of Jesus given in the sacred record with any living reality, of which he himself has a conscious experience. He reads that a glorious Sun has come into the moral system of man—he reads and believes the record,—but he does not look for Him, nor expect to find Him, in the moral system of his own experience; nor does he identify the outward account of His movements with anything that he feels and knows within his own heart—for if he did his belief would no longer rest on the outward record, but on his own personal knowledge and experience. And yet Christ is there within him, and the purpose of the outward record is to draw his attention to this living power come into his own nature to bless him there. But he separates the two instead of identifying them, and thus his theory is destitute of life, and his experience is destitute of knowledge.

CHRISTIANITY.

THE reasonableness of a religion seems to me to consist in there being a direct and natural connection between a believing the doctrines which it inculcates and a being formed by these to the character which it recommends. If the belief of the doctrines has no tendency to train the disciple in a more exact and more willing discharge of its moral obligations, there is evidently a very strong probability against the truth of that religion. In other words, the doctrines ought to tally with the precepts, and to contain in their very substance some urgent motives for the performance of them ; because, if they are not of this description, they are of no use. What is the history of another world to me unless it have some intelligible relation to my duties or happiness ? If we apply this standard to the various religions which different nations have framed for themselves, we shall find very little matter for approbation, and a great deal for pity and astonishment. The very States which have chiefly excelled in arts and literature and civil government have failed here most lamentably. Their moral precepts might be very good; but then these precepts had as much connection with the history of astronomy as with the doctrines of their religion. Which of the adventures of Jupiter or Brama or Osiris could be urged as a powerful motive to excite a high moral feeling or to produce a high moral action? The force of the moral precepts was rather lessened than increased by the facts of their mythology. In the religion of Mahomet there are many excellent precepts; but it contains no illustration of the character of God which has any particular tendency beyond or even equal to that of natural religion to enforce these precepts. Indeed, one of the most important doctrines which he taught,—namely, a future life beyond the grave,—from the shape which he gave to it, tended to counteract his moral precepts. He described it as a state of indulgence in sensual gratifications, which never cloyed the appetite; and yet he preached temperance and self-denial. It is evident that any self-restraint which is produced by the belief of this doctrine must be merely external; for the real principle of temperance could not be cherished by the hope of indulgence at a future period. The philosophical systems of theology are no less liable to the charge of absurdity than the popular superstitions. No one can read Cicero's

work on the nature of the gods without acknowledging the justice of the apostle's sentence upon
that class of reasoners,—" professing themselves
to be wise, they became fools."

As the principles and feelings of our nature
which are addressed in religion are precisely the
same with those which are continually exercised in
the affairs of this world, we may expect to find a
resemblance between the doctrines of a true religion
and the means and arguments by which a virtuous
man acquires an influence over the characters and
conduct of his fellow-creatures. When a man
desires another to do anything, that is the precept ;
when he enforces it by any mode of persuasion,
that is the doctrine. When the Athenians were at
war with the Heraclidæ, it was declared by the
Oracle that the nation whose king died first should
be victorious in the contest. As soon as this was
known, Codrus disguised himself, went over to the
camp of the enemy, and exposed himself there to a
quarrel with a soldier, who killed him without knowing who he was. The Athenians sent to demand the
body of their king ; which so alarmed the Heraclidæ,
from the recollection of the Oracle, that they fled in
disorder. Now, let us suppose that Codrus wished
to inculcate the principle of patriotism in his countrymen. If he had merely issued a proclamation com-
manding every citizen to prefer the interest of his

13

country to his own life, he would have been giving them a moral precept, but without a corresponding doctrine. If he had joined to this proclamation the promise of honour and wealth as the rewards of obedience, he would have been adding a very powerful doctrine, yet nevertheless such a doctrine as must have led much more directly to patriotic conduct than to patriotic feeling and principle. Vanity and avarice, without patriotism, might have gained those rewards. But if he wished to excite or to cherish the principle of patriotism in the hearts of his people, he chose the most eloquent and prevailing argument, when he sacrificed his life for them, and thus attracted their admiration and gratitude to that spirit which animated his breast, and their love to that country, of which he was at once the representative and the ransom.

It is indeed a striking and yet an undeniable fact, that we are comparatively little affected by abstract truths in morality. The cry of a child will produce a greater movement, in almost any mind, than twenty pages of unanswerable reasoning. An instinctive acquaintance with this fact guides us in our dealings with our fellow-creatures ; and He who formed the heart of man has attested His revealed word by showing His acquaintance with the channel through which persuasion and instruction might be most effectually communicated.

It may therefore be useful to illustrate at greater length the analogy which exists between the persuasions of the gospel and those which might be fixed on as the most powerful arguments capable of being addressed to any human feelings on the subject of human interests.

Let us, then, present to ourselves a company of men travelling along the seashore. One of them, better acquainted with the ground than the rest, warns them of quicksands, and points out to them a landmark which indicated the position of a dangerous pass. They, however, see no great reason for apprehension; they are anxious to get forwards, and cannot resolve upon making a considerable circuit in order to avoid what appears to them an imaginary evil. They reject his counsel, and proceed onwards. In these circumstances, what argument ought he to use? What mode of persuasion can we imagine fitted to fasten on their minds a strong conviction of the reality of their danger, and the disinterested benevolence of their adviser? His words have been ineffectual; he must try some other method; he must act. And he does so; for, seeing no other way of prevailing on them, he desires them to wait only a single moment, till they see the truth of his warning confirmed by his fate. He goes before them; he puts his foot on the seemingly firm sand, and sinks to death.

This eloquence is irresistible : He was the most active and vigorous amongst them; if anyone could have extricated himself from the difficulty, it was he ; they are persuaded ; they make the necessary circuit, bitterly accusing themselves of the death of their generous companion ; and during their progress, as often as these landmarks occur, his nobleness and their own danger rise to their minds, and secure their safety. Rashness is not now perilous merely,—it is ungrateful ; it is making void the death of their deliverer.

To walk without God in the world is to walk in sin ; and sin is the way of danger. Men had been told this by their own consciences, and they had even partially and occasionally believed it ; but still they walked on. Common arguments had failed ; the manifestations of the Divine character in creation and providence, and the testimony of conscience, had been in a great measure disregarded ; it thus seemed necessary that a stronger appeal should be made to their understanding and their feelings. The danger of sin must be more strikingly and unequivocally demonstrated ; and the alarm excited by this demonstration must be connected with a more kindly and generous principle, which may bind their affections to that God from whom they have wandered. But how is this to be done ; what more prevailing appeal can be made ? Must the Almighty Warner demonstrate the evil of sin by undergoing its effects? Must He prove the danger of sin by exhibiting Himself as a sufferer under its consequences? Must He who knew no sin suffer as a sinner, that He might persuade men that sin is indeed an evil?—It was even so. God became man, and dwelt amongst us. He Himself encountered the terrors of guilt, and bore its punishment; and called on His careless creatures to consider and understand the evil of sin, by contemplating even its undeserved effects on a being of perfect purity, who was over all, God blessed for ever. Could they hope to sustain that weight which had crushed the Son of God? Could they rush into that guilt and that danger against which He had so pathetically warned them? Could they refuse their hearts and their obedience to Him who had proved Himself so worthy of their confidence?—especially when we consider that this great Benefactor is ever present, and sees the acceptance which this history of His compassion meets with in every breast, rejoicing in those whose spirits are purified by it, and still holding out the warning of His example to the most regardless.

Ancient history tells us of a certain king who made a law against adultery, in which it was enacted that the offender should be punished by the loss of both eyes. The first offender was his

own son.   The case was most distressing ; for the
king was an affectionate father as well as a just
magistrate.   After much deliberation and inward
struggle, he finally commanded one of his own eyes
to be pulled out and one of his son's.   It is easier
to conceive than to describe what must have been
the feelings of the son in these most affecting
circumstances.   His offence would appear to him
in a new light ; it would appear to him not simply
as connected with painful consequences to himself,
but as the cause of a father's sufferings, and as an
injury to a father's love.   If the king had passed
over the law altogether in his son's favour, he
would have exhibited no regard for justice, and he
would have given a very inferior proof of affection.
We measure affection by the sacrifice which it is
prepared to make, and by the resistance which it
overcomes.   If the sacrifice had been made, and
the resistance overcome secretly in the heart of
the king, there could have been but little evidence
of the real existence either of principle or of
affection ; and the son might perhaps have had
reason to think that his pardon was as much the
effect of his father's disregard of the law as of his
affection to him ; and at anyrate, even if he had
given the fullest credit to the abstract justice and
kindness which were combined in his acquittal, it
is impossible that this theoretical character of his

father could have wrought on his heart any impression half so energetic or interesting or over-whelming, as that which must have been produced by the simple and unequivocal and practical exhibi-tion of worth which has been recorded. If we suppose that the happiness of the young man's life depended on the eradication of this criminal propensity, it is not easy to imagine how the king could more wisely or more effectually have promoted this benevolent object. The action was not simply a correct representation of the king's character,—it also contained in itself an appeal most correctly adapted to the feelings of the criminal. It justified the king in the exercise of clemency; it tranquillised the son's mind, as being a pledge of the reality and sincerity of his father's gracious purposes towards him; and it identified the object of his esteem with the object of his gratitude. Mere gratitude, unattracted by an object of moral worth, could never have stamped an impression of moral worth on his character; which was his father's ultimate design. We might suppose the existence of this same character without its producing such an action; we might suppose a conflict of contending feelings to be carried on in the mind, without evidencing, in the conduct flowing from it, the full vehemence of the conflict, or defining the adjustment of the contending feelings; but we cannot suppose any mode of conduct so admirably fitted to impress the stamp of the father's character on the mind of the son, or to associate the love of right and the abhorrence of wrong with the most powerful instincts of the heart. The old man not only wished to act in perfect consistency with his own views of duty, but also to produce a salutary effect on the mind of his son ; and it is the full and effectual union of these two objects which forms the most beautiful and striking part of this remarkable history.

There is a singular resemblance between this moral exhibition and the communication which God has been pleased to make of Himself in the gospel. We cannot but love and admire the character of this excellent prince, although we ourselves have no direct interest in it ; and shall we refuse our love and admiration to the King and Father of the human race, who, with a kindness and condescension unutterable, has, in calling His wandering children to return to duty and to happiness, presented to each of us a like aspect of tenderness and purity, and made use of an argument which makes the most direct and irresistible appeal to the most familiar and at the same time the most powerful principles in the heart of man ?

If Alexander the Great could, by his own skill, have discovered, in the cup presented to him by Philip, certain natural causes restorative of health,

his confidence in the fidelity of his physician would
have had a powerful auxiliary in his own knowledge
of the subject. The conviction of his friend's
integrity was, in his case, however, sufficient by
itself to overcome the suspicions of Parmenio. But
if, by his own knowledge, he had detected anything
in the cup which appeared to him decidedly noxious,
his confidence in his friend would have only led him
to the conclusion that this cup was really not prepared by him; but that some traitor, unobserved
by him, had infused a poisonous ingredient in it.

In like manner, if we discern that harmony in
the Christian revelation which is the stamp of God
upon it, we shall find little difficulty in admitting
that external evidence by which He attested it to
the world. And even though our opportunities or
acquirements do not qualify us for following the
argument in support of miracles, yet if we are convinced that the remedial virtue of its doctrines suits
the necessities and diseases of our nature, we will
not hesitate to assign it to the Great Physician of
souls as its author, nor will we scruple to use it for
our own spiritual health.

No one who knows what God is will refuse to
receive a system of doctrines which he really
believes was communicated by God. But then, no
one in the right exercise of his reason can, by any
evidence, be brought to believe that what appears to

him an absolute absurdity, did ever in truth come from God. At this point the importance of the internal evidence of revelation appears most conspicuous. If any intelligent man has, from hasty views of the subject, received the impression that Christianity is an absurdity, or contains absurdities, he is in a condition to examine the most perfect chain of evidence in its support, with the simple feeling of astonishment at the ingenuity and the fallibility of the human understanding. On a man in this state of mind all arguments drawn from external evidence are thrown away. The thing which he wants is to know that the subject is worth a demonstration ; and this can only be learned by the study of the Bible itself. Let him but give his unprejudiced attention to this book, and he will discover that there is contained in it the development of a mighty scheme, admirably fitted for the accomplishment of a mighty purpose. He will discover that this purpose is no less than to impart to man the happiness of God, by conforming him to the character of God. And he will observe with delight and with astonishment that the grand and simple scheme by which this is accomplished exhibits a system of moral mechanism, which, by the laws of our mental constitution, has a tendency to produce that character, as directly and necessarily as the belief of danger has to produce alarm, the

belief of kindness to produce gratitude, or the belief
of worth to produce esteem. He will discern that
this moral mechanism bears no mark of imposture
or delusion, but consists simply in a manifestation
of the moral character of God, accommodated to the
understandings and hearts of men. And lastly, he
will perceive that this manifestation only gives life
and palpability to that vague though sublime idea
of the Supreme Being, which is suggested by
enlightened reason and conscience.

When a man sees all this in the Bible, his sentiment will be, " I shall examine the evidence in
support of the miraculous history of this book; and
I cannot but hope to find it convincing. But even
should I be left unsatisfied as to the continuity of
the chain of evidence, yet of one thing I am persuaded,—it has probed the disease of the human
heart to the bottom ; it has laid bare the source of
its aberration from moral good and true happiness;
and it has propounded a remedy which carries in
itself the proof of its efficiency. The cause seems
worthy of the interposition of God. He did once
certainly display His own direct and immediate
agency in the creation of the world; and shall I
deem it inconsistent with His gracious character that
He has made another immediate manifestation of
Himself in a work which had for its object the
restoration of innumerable immortal spirits to that

eternal happiness from which, by their moral
depravation, they had excluded themselves?"

There may be also, for anything that the
reasoners of this world know, cycles in the moral
world as well as in the natural; there may be
certain moral conjunctures which, by the Divine
appointment, call for a manifestation of direct
agency from the great First Cause; and in this view
a miraculous interposition, though posterior to the
creation, cannot be considered as an infringement of
the original scheme of things, but as a part and
an essential part of it. When the world was less
advanced in natural science than it is at present,
a comet was considered an infringement on the
original plan. And the period may arrive, and will
assuredly arrive, when the spirits of just men made
perfect shall discern as necessary a connection between the character of God and all the obscurities of
His moral government in our world, as the philosopher now discerns between the properties of matter
and the movements of the various bodies belonging
to our planetary system.

If the gospel really was a communication from
heaven, it was to be expected that it would be
ushered into the world by a miraculous attestation.
It might have been considered as giving a faithful
delineation of the Divine character, although it had
not been so attested; but it could never have

impressed so deep a conviction, nor have drawn such reverence from the minds of men, had it not been sanctioned by credentials which could come from none other than the King of kings. As this conviction and this reverence were necessary to the accomplishment of its moral object, the miracles which produced them were also necessary. Under the name of miraculous attestations, I mean merely those miracles which were extrinsic to the gospel, and did not form an essential part of it; for the greatest miracles of all—namely, the conception, resurrection, and ascension of our Lord—constitute the very substance of the Divine communication, and are essential to the development of that Divine character which gives to the gospel its whole importance.

The belief of the miraculous attestation of the gospel, then, is just so far useful as it excites our reverence for and fixes our attention on the truth contained in the gospel. All the promises of the gospel are to faith in the gospel, and to those moral qualities which faith produces; and we cannot believe that which we do not understand. We may believe that there is more in a thing than we can understand; or we may believe a fact, the causes or modes of which we do not understand; but our actual belief is necessarily limited by our actual understanding. Thus, we understand what we say when we profess our belief that God became man, although we do not understand *how*. This *how*, therefore, is not the subject of belief, because it is not the subject of understanding. We, however, understand *why*—namely, that sinners might be saved, and the Divine character made level to our capacities; and therefore this is a subject of belief. In fact, we can as easily remember a thing which we never knew as believe a thing that we do not understand. In order, then, to believe the gospel, we must understand it; and in order to understand it we must give it our serious attention. An admission of the truth of its miraculous attestation, unaccompanied with a knowledge of its principles, serves no other purpose than to give a most mournful example of the extreme levity of the human mind. It is an acknowledgment that the Almighty took such a fatherly interest in the affairs of men, that He made a direct manifestation of Himself in this world for their instruction; and yet they feel no concern upon the subject of this instruction. Nevertheless, they say, and perhaps think, that they believe the gospel. One of the miraculous appearances connected with our Saviour's ministry places this matter in a very clear light. When, on the Mount of Transfiguration, He for a short time anticipated the celestial glory in the presence of three of His disciples, a voice came from heaven

saying, "This is My beloved Son; *hear ye Him.*"
He was sent to tell men something which they did
not know. Those, therefore, who believed the
reality of this miraculous appearance, and yet did
not listen to what He taught, rejected Him on the
very ground on which it was of prime importance
that they should receive Him.

FAITH

THERE is a fallacy in the idea that the belief of facts is always independent of the will or the moral state of the mind, and therefore out of the reach of praise or blame. When a fact stands closely connected with a general principle, our view of the fact must always be affected by our view of the principle. It is only in this way that we can account for the extraordinary diversity of belief amongst men on the subject of all political facts, such as plots and conspiracies against the government, and the characters of all political men who have filled high situations. There is a diversity of belief not less remarkable on the subject of many moral facts. Some persons seem almost incapable of believing in examples of great generosity and disinterestedness. I can hardly conceive it possible that Nero could believe in a history like that of Codrus, however well supported by evidence. His habits of selfish cruelty must have rendered him impenetrable to such a fact; he could not have comprehended it. And even could it have been demonstrated to him, he would not have believed in its nobleness, but would have laughed at it as an instance of folly or insanity. In many such cases we can predict with tolerable confidence the reception that the recital of certain facts will meet with from certain persons, and we approve or condemn their belief on these occasions, in the same way, and on the same grounds, as we approve or condemn the principles which lead to the belief. The belief in any one of these instances may be at the moment involuntary, that is, it may be the inevitable consequence of a character already formed, but then that character has arisen out of and been confirmed by a series of voluntary actions; and, on this account, we do not feel ourselves to be unjust when we in certain circumstances attach moral praise or blame to a mere belief.

The facts recorded in the Bible are closely connected with important moral principles, and therefore it is to be expected that their general reception or belief will be affected by the estimation in which these principles are held. Those who admit the principles will be disposed to believe the facts, and those who reject the principles will be disposed to disbelieve the facts. But our estimation of moral or spiritual principles is not a thing of indifference—it is that which constitutes the character—it is that on account of which we

14

approve or condemn others, and on account of which we expect to be approved or condemned ourselves. Our belief, then, on such matters is really a part of our moral characters, and liable to moral approbation or disapprobation. We need not wonder, then, that the Bible should speak of faith in its doctrines as a duty, and of unbelief as a sin.

He who knew what was in man, after declaring that "he who believeth on the Son is not condemned, but he that believeth not is condemned already," adds immediately, "and this is the condemnation, that light is come into the world, and men have *loved* darkness rather than light, because their deeds were evil"; thus most explicitly referring belief and unbelief to the state of the heart and affections. But though the sin of the heart is the root of all errors in religion, yet it is of importance to consider those errors separately, that we may know them, and be prepared for them; for it is by blinding our understandings that the deceitfulness of the heart operates.

In the Bible Christianity is given us as a whole; but men are apt to take confined and partial views of it. Faith is connected in Scripture both with the pardon of sin and with the deliverance from the power of sin; or, in other words, with justification and sanctification. In its connexion with justification it is opposed to merit, and desert, and work of every description: "It was by faith that it might be by grace, or gratuitous, or for nothing" (Rom. iv. 16). Some exclusively take this view, which in itself is correct, but which does not embrace the *whole* truth. Faith, as connected with sanctification, "purifieth the heart," "worketh by love," and "overcometh the world," and produces everything which is excellent and holy, as may be seen in that bright roll which is given in Heb. xi. Some again are so engrossed with this view of the subject that they lose sight of the former. This is a fruitful source of error. In order to understand thoroughly the separate parts of a whole, we must understand their connexion with the other parts, and their specific purpose in relation to the whole.

The first of the two classes that have been described call the other *legalists*, or persons who depend on their own performances for acceptance with God. And they are perhaps right in this accusation; but they are not aware that they are very possibly guilty of the same offence. They are almost unconsciously very apt to think that they have paid faith as the price of God's favour. The man who considers faith merely as the channel by which the Divine testimony concerning pardon through the blood of the Lamb is conveyed to his understanding, and operates on his heart, cannot look on faith as a work, because he views it merely as the inlet by which spiritual light enters his soul. Whilst he who considers the declaration, "he that believeth shall be saved," as expressing the arbitrary condition on which pardon will be bestowed, without referring to its natural effects on the character, requires to be very much on his guard indeed against a dependence on his faith as a meritorious act. He will not, to be sure, speak of it in this way, but he runs great risk of feeling about it in this way. And it is not unworthy of observation that those whose statements in this respect have been the highest, have often, in their controversies, assumed towards their opponents a tone of bitterness and contempt most unbecoming the Christian character. This looks like self-righteousness, and seems to mark that they are trusting rather in their own faith, which elevates them, than in the cross of Christ, which would humble them.

In like manner, the second of these classes charge the other with antinomianism, though they themselves are liable to the same charge. They hate the name of antinomianism, and they wish to escape from it as far as possible, but they mistake the way. They are so much occupied with the Christian character that they forget the doctrine of free grace, by the influence of which doctrine alone that character can be formed. They endeavour to become holy by sheer effort. Now this is impossible. They

can never love God by merely trying to love Him,
nor can they hate sin by merely trying to hate it.
The belief of the love of God to sinners, and of the
evil of sin, as manifested in the cross of Christ, can
alone accomplish this change within them.   Those
who substitute effort for the gospel preach antinomianism, because they preach a doctrine which can
never, in the nature of things, lead to the fulfilment
of the law.

Another great source of error on this subject
has been the idea that the importance of faith consists rather in the act of belief than in the object
believed.   Those who entertain this idea look on
faith merely as one part of that manifold obedience
which they owe to God; they consider it simply as
an act of homage to Him, or as a prostration of
their reason before His authority; and they think
that they fulfil their duty on this point when they
entertain no doubts as to the inspiration of the
Bible, and when they do not presume to question
anything contained in it, however little they may
comprehend its meaning.   There cannot be any
greater delusion than this, that merit may consist
in the renunciation of reason, or that the intelligent
and gracious Being "who teacheth man knowledge,"
should require of him, as an act of obedience, that
he should profess his belief in something, he knows
not what, and he knows not why.   There are two

radical mistakes in this view of the subject. The first is, the idea that faith can be exercised without the concurrence of the understanding, when it is evidently through the medium of the understanding alone that we can know either what we believe or what we disbelieve; the second is, the idea that pardon is given as a reward for our believing or for our doing anything else. Pardon is a free gift to man, conveyed and proclaimed through the sacrifice of Jesus Christ. What, then, it may be asked, is the use of faith at all in relation to pardon? The answer is easy. A great part of the punishment of sin consists in the disorder of the thoughts and feelings produced by sin; and therefore the pardon, to be effectual, must reach the thoughts and feelings; that is to say, it must be understood and felt, or, in other words, believed. A good deal of this evil is to be attributed to the technical language in which this subject has been discussed.

Theological writers have distinguished and described different kinds of faith, as speculative and practical—historical, saving, and realising faith. It would be of little consequence what names we gave to faith, or to anything else, provided these names did not interfere with the distinctness of our ideas of the things to which they are attached; but as we must be sensible that they do very much interfere with these ideas, we ought to be on our guard

against any false impressions which may be received
from an incorrect use of them.   Is it not evident
that this way of speaking has a natural tendency
to draw the attention away from *the thing to be
believed*, and to engage it in a fruitless examination of
the *mental operation of believing*?   And, accordingly,
is it not true that we see and hear of more anxiety
amongst religious people about their faith being of
the right kind, than about their believing the right
things?   A sincere man, who has never questioned
the Divine authority of the Scripture, and who can
converse and reason well on its doctrines, yet finds
perhaps that the state of his mind and the tenor of
his life do not agree with the Scripture rule.   He
is very sensible that there is an error somewhere,
but instead of suspecting that there is something in
the very essentials of Christian doctrine which he
has never yet understood thoroughly, the probability
is that he, and his advisers, if he ask advice, come
to the conclusion that his faith is of a wrong kind,
that it is speculative or historical, and not true
saving faith.   Of course this conclusion sends him,
not to the study of the Bible, but to the investiga-
tion of his own feelings, or rather of the laws of his
own mind.   He leaves that truth which God has
revealed and blessed as the medicine of our natures,
and bewilders himself in a metaphysical labyrinth.

The Bible is throughout a practical book, and

never, in all the multitude of cases which it sets
before us for our instruction, does it suppose it
possible for a man to be ignorant or in doubt
whether he really believes or not. It speaks indeed
of faith unfeigned, in opposition to a hypocritical
pretence—and it speaks of a dead faith when it
denies the existence of faith altogether. We deny
the existence of benevolence, argues the apostle,
when fair words are given instead of good offices;
even so we may deny the existence of faith when it
produces no fruit, and merely vents itself in professions; in such a case faith is departed, it is no
more, it is dead; there is a carcass, to be sure, to be
seen, but the spirit is gone. In the place to which
I am now referring, namely, in the second chapter
of James, the writer gives another account of dead
faith, which is very important; it occurs in the 19th
verse. This faith he calls dead because it relates
to an object which, when taken alone, can produce
no effect upon our minds: "Thou believest that
there is one God; thou dost well: the devils also
believe, and tremble." Now the mere belief of the
unity of the Godhead, however important when
connected with other truths, cannot of itself make a
man either better or happier. What feeling or act
is there which springs directly from a belief of the
unity of the Godhead? When connected with other
things it does produce effects; thus the devils con-

nect it with a belief in the avenging justice of God, and hence they tremble, because there is no other God, no other power to appeal to. Christians connect it with a belief in the love of God through the Redeemer, and hence they have good hope, for none can pluck them out of His hands. But the abstract belief that there is one God leads to nothing. It is the belief which we have of the *moral character* of God which can alone influence our characters. After having learned the doctrine of His unity, the great questions still remain, How do we stand in relation to this one great Being? How does He regard us? What does He love, and what does He condemn? These are the great questions in religion; and the Trinitarian who does not find their answer in the doctrine of the Trinity is certainly little benefited by his professed belief on this point.

It is not an easy, because it is not a natural exercise of the mind, to look into itself and to examine its various susceptibilities and the mode or law according to which these are excited by external objects; and whilst we are engaged in this manner we must necessarily remain to a great degree unaffected by those external objects, which we are using merely as parts of the apparatus required for making the experiment on our own faculties. We must endeavour to be in some degree affected by them, in order that we may observe the mode in which they affect us; but that degree will necessarily be very inconsiderable, in consequence of our attention being chiefly directed towards our own feelings. If I am intent on examining and investigating the pleasing emotion which is produced in the mind by the contemplation of the beauties of nature, it is impossible that I can feel much of that pleasure. I may be surrounded by all that is sublime and all that is lovely in creation, but I remain unmoved if, instead of being occupied with the scene before me, I am engaged in a metaphysical examination of my own emotions. The delightful feeling is produced by contemplating the external object—not by observing nor by knowing *how* we enjoy it. The more thoroughly we are occupied by the object, the more thoroughly will our pleasurable susceptibilities be excited; and the more interrupted and distracted our contemplation of the object is, the more inconsiderable will be the gratification arising from it. We cannot excite the pleasing emotion by mere effort, without the real or imagined presence of its natural exciting object; and whilst we attempt to analyse the origin and progress of the emotion, the object fades from our view, and the sensation dies along with it. Our minds are in this respect like mirrors, and the impressions made on them resemble the images reflected by mirrors. No effort of ours can produce an image in the mirror, independent of its proper corresponding object. When that object is placed before it, the image appears, and when it is withdrawn the image disappears. And if, in the minuteness of our examination of the image, we look too narrowly into the mirror, we may find that we have interposed ourselves between the mirror and the object; and that, instead of the image which we expected, our own face is all that we can discover. I beg the reader to bear in mind that these observations do not at all interfere with the Christian duty of self-examination, which relates not to the philosophy of the human mind, but to the actual state of the human heart.

The science of the human mind requires this reflex exertion, because its object is to examine and discover the laws according to which the mind acts or is acted upon; but Christianity requires no such act, because its object is not to discover the laws according to which the mind is impressed, but actually to make impressions on the mind by presenting to it objects fitted and destined for this purpose by Him who made the mind and fixed its laws. The objects of religion were not revealed to us to sharpen our faculties by observing how they were fitted to impress the mind, but that our minds might really be impressed by them with the characters of happiness and holiness. These characters are the subjects of self-examination, and

they are all contained in the Divine precepts.   Do
we love God and our neighbour, and do we give
proof of the reality of our love by corresponding
action ?   This is a very different process from that
to which I am referring.   My object is to point out
the folly of attempting or expecting to make any
impressions on our minds by mere effort, instead of
bringing them into contact with those objects which
God has made known to us in the gospel as the
proper means of producing these impressions—
and especially to warn against that particular
species of this general error, which consists in considering rather *how* we believe than *what* we believe.

Those who oppose the doctrine of justification by
faith without works suppose that pardon, or heaven,
which they conceive to be the same thing as
pardon, is given as a premium for believing the
gospel, or even perhaps as a premium for surrender-
ing their own reason to the authority of the Divine
revelation.   I ask whether this is not the common
notion of those who oppose the doctrine of justification by faith ?   I am persuaded that it is, and
I can at the same time affirm that there is not
the slightest foundation for such a notion in any
scriptural statement of the doctrine.   Christianity
holds out no premium for faith at all which is not
consistent with the common sense and the common
experience of mankind.   If I find a mother weeping

over the account of the death of her firstborn,
which I know to be a false report, am I to be
considered as a very adventurous prophet, or
extravagant promiser, if, when I lay before her the
proof of his being in perfect health, I make the
declaration beforehand, that if she believes my news
she will be saved from her sorrow, and that her
heart will rejoice? Why, this is no more than what
every reasonable being must regard as the necessary
consequence of such a belief. Yet it is true that
she is saved from her anguish by faith in my story.
But her joy is not a premium bestowed on her to
reward her belief; it flows naturally out of her
belief. Her grief for the supposed death of her
child, and her belief that he is alive and well,
cannot exist in her mind together. Such a faith
necessarily heals such a sorrow. Her faith does
not restore her son to life,—he is alive whether she
believes it or not,—but his life is no joy to her
unless she believes it. Without faith in my story
she could not be saved from her distress. Take
another example. A son outrages in a most
atrocious manner the feelings of his father. The
father banishes him from his house, after pronounc-
ing a malediction on him. The son hears of his
death soon after, and feels his spirit burdened with
the curse; he cannot shake himself free of it—he
is a miserable wretch. A friend of his father comes

to him and tells him that he had seen his father a few hours before his death, and that he had heard him express the warmest affection for him, and the deepest regret for what had taken place between them ; and that he had received from him a charge to tell him that he had withdrawn his curse, and had prayed a blessing on him. The son receives the intelligence with grateful joy, and his burden drops from him. *He is saved by faith.* His mind is healed by believing the information which has been given him. His father's forgiveness is not given him as a reward of his believing this history ; but unless he believes it, the forgiveness is quite useless to him—he will continue to feel his father's curse clinging to him.

But let me now here suppose for a moment that the friend, instead of simply relating to him the fact of his father's forgiveness, had put the whole history into the form under which the gospel is very often preached,—suppose he had said to him, your father has forgiven you, if you believe in my testimony of his forgiveness ; but if you cannot do this there is no forgiveness for you. One can easily imagine the perplexity into which the son would be thrown by such an announcement. It would appear to him as if the truth of a past fact depended on the state of his feeling with regard to it. It would be impossible for him, in such circumstances, to believe, because his informant actually told him that his belief of the pardon must precede the existence of the pardon.

I have not here supposed the existence of any penalty or positive infliction attending the curse which might be removed by the forgiveness. I have considered it only as the means of relieving a mental distress. In this latter view it is quite evident to common sense that faith in the forgiveness is necessary in order to give it any efficacy. But if there be positive inflictions or penalties to be removed by the pardon, this effect may be produced altogether independently of faith in the pardon. Thus, had the father disinherited his son, and then cancelled the deed, the son's right of succession would not have been at all affected by his belief or unbelief of his father's forgiveness.

In like manner, had the evils under which man labours consisted merely in external penalties and judicial inflictions, his faith in the forgiveness which removed them would never have been required, because his faith gives no efficacy to the pardon in this respect. But if a great part of the misery of sin consists in the diseased condition of the mind produced by it—if it consists mainly in the state of the thoughts and feelings, then a pardon which would deliver from this misery must address and enter the thoughts and feelings; that is to say, it must be understood and felt—and how can it be so, unless it is believed ?

The use of faith, then, is not to remove the penalty, or to make the pardon better,—for the penalty is removed and the pardon is proclaimed, whether we believe it or not,—but to give the pardon a moral influence, by which it may heal the spiritual diseases of the heart; which influence it cannot have in the nature of things unless it is believed. When a messenger from heaven made known to the shepherds of Bethlehem that the Saviour was born, and that through Him peace was proclaimed on earth, and goodwill from God to man, the truth of the fact, and the sincerity of that goodwill which the Creator thus manifested towards His creatures, did not depend at all on the faith of the shepherds; but their own spiritual healing, as far as it was connected with joy and gratitude and hope, depended entirely on their belief of the message.

Men are not, according to the gospel system, pardoned on account of their belief of the pardon; but they are sanctified by a belief of the pardon. And unless the belief of it produces this effect, neither the pardon nor the belief are of any use. The use of a medicine is to restore health; if it does not accomplish this it is useless. The pardon of the gospel is a spiritual medicine—faith is no-

thing more than the taking of that medicine ; and if
spiritual health or sanctification is not produced,
neither the spiritual medicine nor the taking of the
medicine are of any avail; they have failed in their
object.

Even had there been no mention of faith made
through the whole Bible, it is yet evident to
common sense that its communications could be
profitable to none but to those who believed them;
and it is no less evident that unless these communications are understood, they cannot be believed in
their true meaning.   Our business, then, is to
understand the meaning of these communications,
and to receive them as substantial realities, altogether independent of our admission or rejection.
Certain facts have taken place, and certain principles
exist in the government of the universe, whether we
believe them or not.   Our disbelief of them neither
destroys their existence nor takes from their
importance ; they continue the same, and will
continue to exercise an unlimited and uncontrollable
influence over our destinies for ever.   These facts
and principles declare the character of God, and it
is life eternal to know them.   To reject them is to
clash with Omnipotence ; and to be ignorant of
them is to be in moral darkness.

We must prosecute our inquiries on this subject,
not as critics or judges or scholars, but as sinners.

15

It is not an interesting exercise for our faculties, but a pardon for our sins and a cure for our spiritual diseases, that we must seek after. If we seek we shall find, and we shall find them in Jesus Christ. But the discovery, though it will gladden, will not elate. The great end for which we are called on to believe the gospel is that we may be conformed by it to the likeness of Him who was meek and lowly in heart. Our obedience to the law of God is thus the measure of our faith in the gospel.

THE ATONEMENT

THE doctrine of the atonement through Jesus Christ, which is the corner-stone of Christianity, and to which all the other doctrines of revelation are sub-servient, has had to encounter the misapprehension of the understanding as well as the pride of the heart. This pride is natural to man, and can only be overcome by the power of the truth. But the misapprehension might be removed by the simple process of reading the Bible with attention, because it has arisen from neglecting the record itself, and taking our information from the discourses or the systems of men who have engrafted the meta-physical subtilties of the schools upon the unper-plexed statement of the Word of God. In order to understand the facts of revelation, we *must* form a system to ourselves; but if any subtilty, of which the application is unintelligible to common sense or uninfluential on conduct, enters into our system, we may be sure that it is a wrong one. The common-sense system of a religion consists in two connexions—first, the connexion between the doctrines and the character of God which they exhibit; and, secondly, the connexion between these same doctrines and the character which they are intended to impress on the mind of man. When, therefore, we are considering a religious doctrine, our questions ought to be—first, What view does this doctrine give of the character of God in relation to sinners? And, secondly, What influence is the belief of it calculated to exercise on the character of man? Though I state the questions separately, my observations on them cannot properly be kept entirely distinct. The first of these questions leads us to consider the atonement as an act necessarily resulting from and simply developing principles in the Divine mind, altogether independent of its effects on the hearts of those who are interested in it. The second leads us to consider the adaptation of the history of the atonement, when believed, to the moral wants and capacities of the human mind. This last consideration opens a field of most interesting inquiry, and the deeper we search into it the stronger reasons shall we discover for admiration and gratitude, and the more thoroughly shall we be convinced that this adaptation does not resemble the petty and precarious and temporising adjustments of human policy; but that it is stamped with the uncounterfeited seal of the universal Ruler, and carries on it the traces of that same mighty will which has adapted the properties of the great luminary of our system to the physical wants and capacities of the various tribes of being which inhabit the earth. Yet it must be remembered that this adaptation is only an evidence for the truth of the gospel, but that it does not constitute the gospel. The gospel consists in the proclamation of mercy through the sacrifice of Jesus Christ. This is the only true source of sanctity and peace and hope; and if, instead of drinking from this fountain, we busy ourselves in tracing the course of the streams that flow from it, and in admiring the beauty and fertility of the country through which they run, we may indeed have a tasteful and sentimental relish for the organisation of Christianity; but it will not be in us a well of water springing up into ever-lasting life. Before we admit the truth of a doctrine like the atonement, it is proper to contemplate it in all its consequences; but after we have admitted it we ought to give the first place in our thoughts to the doctrine itself, because our minds are usefully operated on, not by the thought of the consequences, but by the contemplation of the doctrine. When an act of kindness has been done to us, our gratitude is excited by contemplating the kindness itself, not by investigating that law in our nature by which gratitude naturally

is produced by kindness.   It is of great importance
to remember this.   We do not, and cannot, become
Christians by thinking of the Christian character,
nor even by thinking of the adaptation of the
Christian doctrines to produce that character, but
by having our hearts impressed and imbued by the
doctrines themselves.   The doctrines are constituent
parts of God's character and government, and they
are revealed to us that we may be renewed in
the spirit of our minds by the knowledge of
them.

The doctrine of the atonement is the great
subject of revelation.   God is represented as
delighting in it, as being glorified by it, and as
being most fully manifested by it.   All the other
doctrines radiate from this as their centre.   In
subservience to it, the distinction in the unity of
the Godhead has been revealed.   It is described
as the everlasting theme of praise and song amongst
the blessed who surround the throne of God.   It is
represented in language suitable to our capacities,
as calling forth all the energies of omnipotence.
And, indeed, when we come to consider what this
great work was, we shall not wonder that even the
inspired heralds of salvation faultered in the utterance of it.   The human race had fallen off from
their allegiance, they had turned away from God,
their hearts chose what God abhorred, and despised

what God honoured. They were the enemies of God, they had broken His law which their own consciences acknowledged to be holy, just, and gracious, and had thus most righteously incurred the penalty denounced against sin. Man had thus ruined himself, and the faithfulness of God seemed bound to make this ruin irretrievable.

The design of the atonement was to make mercy towards this offcast race consistent with the honour and the holiness of the Divine government. To accomplish this gracious purpose, the Eternal Word, who was God, took on Himself the nature of man, and as the elder brother and representative and champion of the guilty family, He solemnly acknowledged the justice of the sentence pronounced against sin, and submitted Himself to its full weight of woe in the stead of His adopted kindred. God's justice found rest here; His law was magnified and made honourable. The human nature of the Saviour gave Him a brother's right and interest in the human race, whilst His Divine nature made His sacrifice available, and invested the law under which He had bowed Himself with a glory beyond what could have accrued to it from the penal extinction of a universe. The two books of the Bible in which this subject is most minutely and methodically argued, namely, the Epistles to the Romans and the Hebrews, commence with assert-

ing most emphatically both the perfect divinity
and the perfect humanity of Jesus Christ. On
this basis the reasoning is founded which demon-
strates the universal sufficiency and the suitableness of the death of Christ as an atonement for
the sins of men, or as a vindication of the justice of
the Divine government in dispensing mercy to the
guilty.   What a wonderful and awful and enliven-
ing subject of contemplation this is ! " God *so* loved
the world, that He gave His only begotten Son, that
whosoever believeth on Him might not perish, but
have everlasting life."   And the same God, that He
might declare His abhorrence of sin in the very
form and substance of His plan of mercy, sent
forth this Son to make a propitiation *through His
blood*.   This is the God with whom we have to do.
This is His character, the Just God and yet the
Saviour.   There is an augustness and a tenderness
about this act, a depth and height and breadth
and length of moral worth and sanctity which
defies equally the full grasp of thought and of
language ; but we can understand something of it,
and therefore has it been revealed to us.   But does
it not mark in most fearful contrast the difference
which exists between the mind of God and the
mind of man ?   Whilst man is making a mock at
sin, God descends from the throne of glory and
takes on Him the frailty of a creature, and dies as a

creature the representative of sinners, before His holy nature can pronounce sin forgiven. It was to remove this difference that these glad tidings have been preached; and he that believes this history of God shall be like Him, for in it he sees God as He is. In this wonderful transaction mercy and truth meet together, righteousness and peace embrace each other. It was planned and executed in order that God might be just whilst He justified the believer in Jesus. It proclaims glory to God in the highest, peace on earth and goodwill to man. The new and divinely constituted Head of the human family has been raised from the dead, His sacrifice has been judicially accepted, and He has been crowned with immortality in His representative character. This is the foundation on which sinners are invited to rest the interests of their souls for eternity. It is held up for their most scrutinising inspection, and they are urged to draw near and examine whether it be sufficient to bear their weight. They are asked, as it were, if they can discover a flaw in the fulness and sincerity and efficiency of that love which could prompt God to veil His majesty, and ally Himself with our polluted race, and assume an elder brother's interest in our welfare, and magnify the law which we had broken, by suffering its penalty in our room, and thus connect the Divine glory with the salvation of sinners. They are assured on the authority of God that the blood of Christ cleanseth from all sin, and that there is no condemnation to those who believe on Him. They have thus the declaration of God, and the act of God, still more impressive and persuasive than His declaration, to engage their confidence and to banish all doubts and suspicions from their breasts. As the Saviour expired on the cross, He said, "It is finished." The work of expiation was then accomplished; and the history of that work comes forth in the form of a general address to the sons of men, "Return unto Me, for I have redeemed you." "Be ye reconciled to God." This is the fountain of the river of life, and over it are these words written, "Ho, every one that thirsteth, come ye to the waters." It proclaims pardon for sin; it is therefore quite suited for sinners. Jesus came not to call the righteous, but sinners to repentance; He came to seek and to save that which was lost. He said this Himself, and He said it whilst every possible variety and aggravation of guilt stood full in the view of His omniscience. He said it whilst He was contemplating that cup of bitterness and amazement and death which He had engaged to drink, and which was mixed for Him to this very end, that the chief of sinners might be welcomed to the water of life.

What is that weight of guilt which can exclude from mercy ? The very thought is degrading to the dignity of the sacrifice, and injurious to the holy love which appointed it, and to the unstained truth which has pronounced its all-sufficiency. Can we wonder, then, at the high-toned triumph which filled the soul of the Apostle Paul as he gazed on this glorious object, and saw in it the pledge that his sins, which were many, were forgiven him, and that the heart of his often outraged Master yearned upon him, and that his own lot for eternity was bound up with the glorious eternity of his God ? "Who shall lay any thing to the charge of God's elect ? It is God that justifieth. Who is he that condemneth ? It is Christ that died, yea rather, that is risen again, who is even at the right hand of God, who also maketh intercession for us."

But if the virtue and sufficiency of the atonement be thus universal, why are not the benefits of it universally enjoyed ? Had the mere removal of an impending penalty in consistency with justice constituted the whole and the ultimate object of God in this great work, there would probably have been no difference nor individual peculiarity with respect to these benefits, nor should we have had such admonitions addressed to us as the following : "Many are called, but few are chosen;" "work out your own salvation with fear and trembling;" "do all diligence to make your calling and election sure." But Christ gave Himself for us, not only to redeem us from the punishment due to iniquity, but also that He might purify to Himself a peculiar people zealous of good works. The subjects of His kingdom were to be those in whose hearts *the truth* dwelt, the great truth relating to the character of God. This truth was developed and exhibited in the atonement—its bright rays were concentrated there ; and therefore the intelligent belief of the atonement was the most proper channel through which this Divine light might enter the soul of man. It is this light alone which can chase away the shades of moral darkness, and restore life and spiritual vigour to the numbed and bewildered faculties. And therefore the benefits of the atonement are connected with a belief of the atonement. "He that believeth shall be saved ; he that believeth not shall be condemned." When the identity of unhappiness and moral darkness in an intelligent subject of God's government is fully understood, this connexion between belief and salvation will appear to be not the appointment of a new enactment, but merely the renewed declaration of an established and necessary constitution. The truth concerning God's character is an immortal and glorious principle, developed and laid up in Jesus Christ; and God imparts its immortality and glory to the spirits in which it dwells. This truth cannot dwell in us except in so far as the work of Christ remains as a reality in our minds. We cannot enjoy the spiritual life and peace of the atonement separated from the believing remembrance of the atonement, as we cannot enjoy the light of the sun separated from the presence of the sun. It would be a foolish madness to think of locking in the light by shutting our casements, and it is no less foolish to dream of appropriating the peace of the gospel whilst the great truth of the gospel is not in the eye of faith. In the Epistle to the Galatians, v. 25, St. Paul says, if ye have your life from the gospel (here called the Spirit), see that you walk in, *i.e.* keep close to, the Spirit. When our hearts stray from the truth, we stray from that life which is contained in the truth. We cannot long continue or retain any moral impression on our minds separate from the object which is fitted to produce the impression.

The man who sees in the atonement a deliverance from ruin, and a pledge of immortal bliss, will rejoice in it, and in all the principles which it develops. "Let not the wise man," says the prophet, "glory or rejoice in his wisdom, neither let the mighty man rejoice in his might, let not the rich man rejoice in his riches; but let him that rejoiceth rejoice in this, that he understandeth and knoweth Me, that I am the Lord which exercise loving-kindness, judgment, and righteousness, in the earth : for in these things I delight, saith the Lord." He therefore who rejoices in the atonement rejoices in that which delights the heart of God; for here have His loving-kindness and His judgment and His righteousness been most fully and most gloriously exercised. It is thus that the believer has communion with God through Jesus Christ, and it is thus that he becomes conformed to His moral likeness. The same truth which gives peace produces also holiness. What a view does the cross of Christ give of the depravity of man, and of the guilt of sin! And must not the abhorrence of it be increased tenfold by the consideration that it has been committed against the God of all grace and of all consolation? A sense of our interest would keep us close to that Saviour in whom our life is treasured up, if we needed such a motive to bind us to a Benefactor who chose to bear the wrath of Omnipotence rather than that we should bear it. Shall we frustrate the designs of love by our own undoing, and trample on that sacred blood which was shed for us ? No; if we believe in the atonement, we must love Him who made the atonement; and if we love Him, we shall enter into His views, we shall feel for the honour of God, we shall feel for the souls of men, we shall loath sin especially in our own hearts, we shall look forward with an earnestness of expectation to the period when the mystery of God shall be finished and the spiritual temple completed and the Redeemer's triumph fulfilled. This hope we have as an anchor of the soul sure and steadfast; it is fixed within the vail; it looks to the atonement; and whatever be the afflictions or the trials of life, it can still rejoice in that voice which whispers from the inner sanctuary, "be of good cheer, it is I, be not afraid"; it can still feel the force of that reasoning, "He that spared not His own Son, but gave Him up for us all, how shall He not with Him freely also give us all things?" This hope maketh not ashamed, it will not and cannot disappoint, because it is founded on the character of that God who changeth not.

It is thus that the faith of the gospel produces that revolution in the mind which is called in Scripture conversion or the new birth. A man naturally trusts to something within himself, to his prudence, or to his good fortune, or to his worth, or to his acquirements, or to what he has done well, or to his unfeigned sorrow for what he has done ill; self, in one form or other more or less amiable, is the foundation of his hope, and by

necessary consequence self is ever present to his
view, and becomes the ultimate object of his
conduct, and the director and the former of his
character. But when he believes and understands
the truth of God as manifested in the atonement
to be the only foundation on which he can rest
with safety, the only refuge from that ruin into
which he has been led by the guidance of self, he
will cast from him these perishing and fluctuating
delusions, and he will repose his interests for time
and for eternity on the love of Him who bled for
him, and on the faithfulness of Him who is not
a man that He should lie, nor the Son of Man that
He should repent; and resting thus on the character of God as the exclusive ground of his
confidence, he will contemplate it as his ultimate
object, he will cleave to it as his counsellor and
his guide, and will thus be gradually moulded into
its likeness. This foundation of hope continues the
same through every stage of the Christian's progress.
Though his growth in personal sanctity be the
grand and blessed result of his faith, yet that
sanctity can never become the ground of his confidence without throwing him back upon self, and
separating him from God and cutting off his supply
from the living fountain of holiness, and thus
unsanctifying him. But although personal sanctity
can never become the foundation of hope, yet it

will much strengthen our confidence in that foundation; just as returning health strengthens the confidence of the patient in that medicine which he feels restoring him.

A man's character is formed by his habitual impressions or prevalent objects of thought and feeling. Let us suppose a person of good natural affections to have his mind occupied continually by the history of an injurious fraud which he believes to have been practised against him on some occasion. It is impossible that he can escape being miserable and becoming morally depraved. His bad passions, by being constantly excited, must grow in strength and in susceptibility of similar impressions, and his happier affections, by being unexercised, must fade and die. Let us again suppose a man with less amiable natural qualities, whose life or fortune had been at one time saved by the self-sacrificing generosity of a friend. If this event makes such an impression on him as to be more present to his thoughts than any other, it cannot fail of softening and improving his character and increasing his happiness. His good affections are thus continually exercised, and must therefore be continually gaining strength, whilst bad passions are at the same time displaced. Of those who have acquired the character of misanthropes, probably nine out

16

of ten have, like Timon, been men of generous dispositions, who, having been deceived in friendship,
have ever after looked on fair professions as the
symbols of dishonest intentions.   Their feelings of
contempt and hatred and wounded pride, being
thus continually exercised by this unfortunate
belief, the whole frame of their character has been
ruined, and their peace of mind destroyed.   And
it is possible that, if we could look into the hearts
of men and trace their history, we might find
some of the brightest examples of benevolence
amongst those whose natural dispositions were
most opposite to it, but who had allowed the
history of the Redeemer's love so to abide in them,
that it had softened and changed their hearts, and
healed their diseased affections.   If, then, the
importance of the gospel is perceived, it will
occupy the mind much; and if it does so, it will
give the faculties a right direction, and keep them
in healthful exercise.

There are many who consider the atonement
by Christ merely as a means of procuring the
pardon of sin.   But this is a very limited and
erroneous view of the subject.   Its relation to
holiness and obedience is as near as its relation to
pardon.   It contains a medicine for the mind, and
a direct and fitting and salutary object for all its
faculties.   What poor shrunken things the minds

of men in general are! our noblest powers are,
for the most part, either left altogether without an
object, or directed to wrong ones. Far from being
kept in ennobling and worthy employment, to the
stretching and unfolding of their high capacities,
and the fulfilment of the glorious destinies for
which they were bestowed, they are forced to con-
tract and narrow themselves, in order to approach
and embrace the paltry objects to which they are
most unequally mated. The conscience, by being
directed merely to external duties and social cere-
monies, becomes blind to the excellence of spiritual
truth ; the affections, by being attached solely to
created things, become polluted, and introduce
tumult and disorder into the mind, because they
can find no fitting rest; and the principle of
prudence is degraded down to ambition and
avarice and every meanness, because it is not
taught to look to God as the source of all real
happiness. This disordered state of the mind constitutes its misery, and assuredly also constitutes
much of the punishment of sin. A pardon, which
left this disorder unremedied, would leave our
punishment unremoved. External and judicial
inflictions might be withdrawn or remitted, but the
mind would still continue to be its own tormentor,
its own hell. The pardon, to be adequate to our
wants, should heal this spiritual disorder. The

disorder consists in the misdirection of the faculties to improper and hurtful objects; the cure, therefore, must consist in leading them back and fixing them on their true objects. This is the great design of the gospel. In the history of the atonement, the character of God is set before us as the healthful and satisfying and expanding object of all our faculties. The conscience is enlightened, as it contemplates the majestic spectacle of the Deity, veiling as it were His omnipotence before the claims of duty, and merging His high prerogative of sovereignty in the qualities of justice and mercy. I may be permitted to speak the language of human feeling on this subject, so that I speak humbly. The revelation is addressed to human thought and human feeling; and a superstitious dread of approaching it or scrutinising it, though not so impious as a light familiarity, is still a sin against its purpose and its use.

To speak, then, in the language of men; God, as far as our thoughts can carry, could have pardoned sin without an atonement; His right of sovereignty and His mercy were both infinite. But it was the Holy God who was acting, and His actions are parts of His character—emanations of His nature. He cannot but express Himself in them. And, as He hates sin, even when He pardons the sinner, so His action expressed this union of

sentiments; and the same fact which proclaimed
mercy condemned sin. There is a glory and a
sublimity of moral worth in this character, which,
when contemplated, must vivify the conscience
and raise its tone, and give edge and weight to its
approbation of right and its condemnation of
wrong. And what shall we say of this wondrous
theme as an object for the affections? We can
go no farther than to quote the apostle, "Herein
is love." And when the affections are attracted,
think what it is which attracts them. It is not
a kindness merely, it is a high and holy kindness
—it is a wise kindness—it is an eternal kindness.
It is the perfection of moral beauty, an uncreated
loveliness, which, whilst it expands the affections,
purifies and tranquillises them. In like manner,
self-love, or the prudential principle, finds its
object and its repose in the atonement. For
there is revealed in it an unassailable security
under the shadow of the Almighty, and an eternity
of unexpressed joy in the heavenly city promised
under seal of the blood of Christ. And what has
the world to offer in rivalry with these things,
even in the judgment of the most calculating
selfishness?

Thus it is that the mind is healed by faith in
the atonement. Our reason comes in contact with
the wisdom of God—our hopes with His promises

—our desires with His perfections, and the
mysterious imaginings of our hearts with His
infinity. And virtue goes out of Him, and heals
those who touch Him. The gospel then ought
not to be considered as a matter of veneration too
sacred to be touched, not as a mere history of
miraculous occurrences, not as a subject of curious
speculation, but as a repository of the great principles of eternity which God has revealed to us,
that upon them and in them we may stretch and
mould and imbue the faculties of our being.
These principles are high existences which have
been always, and will always be. The facts in
which they have been embodied and manifested
passed in time; they were great and wonderful,
but they have passed—they have passed, but the
principles which they represented remain as young
and vigorous as in the morning of creation. They
know no age; they are the thoughts of Him whose
thoughts are from everlasting. Whilst we converse with them we converse with Him; we
escape from the narrow and dark reign of time
and of decay; we cross the limit which divides the
things which perish from the things which endure;
we are present with all the past and with all the
future—we mingle with eternity. It is by contact and converse with these imperishable and
incorruptible essences that the soul is purified and

invigorated and regenerated through all her powers. It is this contact alone which can do it, and therefore any faculty which does not share in this communion remains unhealed and unblessed.

The objects set before us in the gospel for our belief are a series of facts exhibiting the character of God in relation to man. In order, therefore, to believe them, we must receive on our internal senses, impressions corresponding to this moral meaning, otherwise, although we may believe in their external form, we do not, and cannot believe in their meaning, which constitutes their whole value and importance to us as a revelation. Thus, if a fact is revealed as an exhibition of Divine love, and if I hear it without perceiving this meaning, the fact is really lost on me. I cannot be said to believe in it; for I have received no impression corresponding to its real import on which I might pass a judgment either of belief or disbelief.

The death of Christ, in which all the facts of the gospel meet as their centre, is described as an atonement for the sins of the world, required by infinite holiness, provided by infinite love. "He, by the grace of God, tasted death for every man." "He the one bare the sins of the many." This marks God's judgment of human guilt. The punishment inflicted on the representative measures the deservings of those whose place He filled. It

was an act of justice. " Christ died under the
sentence of sin." This is an address to the conscience, to the sense of right and wrong; and it
is only through the information of the conscience
that we can comprehend it. It was an act of
generous love, of self-sacrifice. " Herein is love,
not that we loved God, but that He loved us,
and sent His Son to be the propitiation for our sins."
It is not a mere picture, nor is it a dictionary which
can explain this to us. To understand it, our souls
must come in contact with the state of alienation
and ruin from which the atonement delivers, and
with the compassion which planned it. It is an
easy matter to repeat words, and to repeat them
without any thought of denying their truth; and
it is no difficult matter to imagine the outward
circumstances of that scene which was acted on
Calvary, without even the shadow of a doubt with
regard to them crossing the mind. But all the
highest faculties of the soul must be called forth,
in order even to form a conception of the meaning
of that declaration, " God so loved the world, that
He gave His only begotten Son, that whosoever
believeth in Him should not perish, but have everlasting life." Here the moral monitor within us
must recognise the nature of sin, and its evil
desert. The affections must strain themselves to
comprehend something of that wondrous love with

which He *so* loved us—our imagination must catch a glimpse of eternity, and our prudential judgment must weigh the two alternatives of *perishing* and *everlasting life*. These principles are the great objects of faith, on account of which the facts are revealed, and without which they would be mere matters of astonishment.

ELECTION

THE doctrine of election generally held is that God, according to His own inscrutable purpose, has from all eternity chosen in Christ, and predestinated unto salvation, a certain number of individuals out of the fallen race of Adam; and that, in pursuance of this purpose, as these individuals come into the world, He in due season visits them by a peculiar operation of His Spirit, thereby justifying and sanctifying and saving them; whilst He passes by the rest of the race, unvisited by that peculiar operation of the Spirit, and so abandoned to their sins and their punishment. It is also an essential part of the doctrine that the peculiar operation of the Spirit, by which God draws the elect unto Himself, is held to be alike irresistible and indispensable in the work of salvation, so that those to whom it is applied cannot be lost, and those to whom it is not applied cannot be saved; whilst all the outward calls of the gospel, and what are named common operations of the Spirit, which are granted to the reprobate as well as to the elect, are, when unaccom-

panied by that peculiar operation, ineffectual to
salvation, and do only aggravate the condemnation
of the reprobate.

I held this doctrine for many years, modified,
however inconsistently, by the belief of God's love
to all, and of Christ having died for all ; and yet,
when I look back on the state of my mind during
that period, I feel that it would be truer to say I
submitted to it, than that I believed it. I submitted to it because I did not see how the language
of the 9th chapter of the Epistle to the Romans,
and of a few similar passages, could bear any other
interpretation ; and yet I could not help feeling
that, on account of what appeared to be the meaning of these few difficult passages, I was giving up
the plain and obvious meaning of all the rest of
the Bible, which seems continually, in the most
unequivocal language and in every page, to say
to every man, " See, I have set before thee this day
life and good, death and evil, therefore choose life
that thou mayest live." I could not help feeling that if the above representation were true, then
that on which a real and righteous responsibility in
man can alone be founded was awanting ; and the
slothful servant had reason, when, in vindication of
his unprofitableness, he said, " I knew thee that
thou art an hard man, reaping where thou hast
not sown, and gathering where thou hast not

strawed." Above all, I could not help feeling
that if God were such as that doctrine described
Him, then the Creator of every man was not the
friend of every man, nor the righteous object of
confidence to every man ; and that when Christ
was preached to sinners, the whole truth of God
was not preached to them, for that there was something behind Christ in the mind of God, giving Him
to one, and withholding Him from another, so that
the ministry of reconciliation was only an appendix
to a deeper and more dominant ministry, in which
God appeared simply as a Sovereign, without any
moral attribute, and man was dealt with as a mere
creature of necessity, without any real responsibility.

I at that time used to answer and rebuke this
doubt of my heart by the words, though, I now see,
not by the meaning of Scripture, "Who art thou
that repliest against God ?" and by the consideration that the finite understanding of man was
incapable of comprehending the infinite mind of
God. But still I remained unsatisfied, because I
met with passages in the Bible in which God
invites and calls upon men to judge of the equality
and righteousness of His ways, placing Himself as it
were at the bar of their consciences, and claiming
from them a judgment testifying to His righteousness, and clearing Him of all inequality, and that
not on the ground that His righteousness is above

their understanding,—far less on the ground that He has a sovereign right to do as He pleases,—but on the ground that His righteousness is such as men can judge of, and because it is clear and plain to that principle of judgment within them, by which they approve or condemn their own actings and the actings of their fellow-men.

The passages to this effect which struck me most forcibly were the 18th and 33rd chapters of Ezekiel, and the 5th chapter of Isaiah. I shall transcribe the greatest part of the 18th of Ezekiel, that I may bring the reader face to face with it. " The word of the Lord came unto me again, saying, What mean ye, that ye use this proverb concerning the land of Israel, saying, The fathers have eaten sour grapes, and the children's teeth are set on edge ? As I live, saith the Lord God, ye shall not have occasion any more to use this proverb in Israel. Behold, all souls are Mine; as the soul of the father, so also the soul of the son is Mine: the soul that sinneth, it shall die." " The son shall not bear the iniquity of the father, neither shall the father bear the iniquity of the son : the righteousness of the righteous shall be upon him, and the wickedness of the wicked shall be upon him. But if the wicked will turn from all his sins that he hath committed, and keep all My statutes, and do that which is lawful and right, he shall surely live,

he shall not die. All his transgressions that he
hath committed, they shall not be mentioned unto
him: in his righteousness that he hath done he
shall live. Have I any pleasure at all that the
wicked should die? saith the Lord God: and not
that he should return from his ways, and live?
But when the righteous turneth away from his
righteousness, and committeth iniquity, and doeth
according to all the abominations that the wicked
man doeth, shall he live? All his righteousness
that he hath done shall not be mentioned: in his
trespass that he hath trespassed, and in his sin that
he hath sinned, in them shall he die. Yet ye say,
The way of the Lord is not equal. Hear now,
O house of Israel; Is not My way equal? are
not your ways unequal? When a righteous
man turneth away from his righteousness, and
committeth iniquity, and dieth in them; for his
iniquity that he hath done shall he die. Again,
when the wicked man turneth away from his
wickedness that he hath committed, and doeth that
which is lawful and right, he shall save his soul
alive. Because he considereth, and turneth away
from all his transgressions that he hath committed,
he shall surely live, he shall not die. Yet saith the
house of Israel, The way of the Lord is not equal.
O house of Israel, are not My ways equal? are not
your ways unequal? Therefore I will judge you,

O house of Israel, every one according to his ways, saith the Lord God. Repent, and turn yourselves from all your transgressions ; so iniquity shall not be your ruin. Cast away from you all your transgressions, whereby ye have transgressed ; and make you a new heart and a new spirit : for why will ye die, O house of Israel ? For I have no pleasure in the death of him that dieth, saith the Lord God : wherefore turn yourselves, and live ye."

It appeared to me impossible to read this passage without perceiving that the *righteousness* of God is assumed throughout to be a righteousness which man is capable of comprehending and appreciating ; and that although His sovereignty is incontestable, He yet, in a manner, holds Himself accountable to the consciences of His intelligent creatures, for the way in which He exercises it.

It further appeared to me that this passage, according to its obvious and natural signification, contained not only a denial of the existence of an eternal purpose of God, by which any of the race of man are passed by and left to their sins and their punishment, but also the assertion of the existence of an opposite purpose in God towards them, even that they should turn from their sins and be saved —and also, that it contained a denial that the difference between the righteous and the wicked arose from God's applying any peculiar irresistible

operation of the Spirit to the former and withholding it from the latter, because such a dealing on the
part of God would destroy the very ground of the
appeal, so strongly urged through the whole chapter,
inasmuch as the intelligible equality of His judgment on both classes depends entirely on the
essential and true sufficiency of the spiritual
provision made for both of them.

It further appeared to me that if men as a race
had, through the fall of Adam, lost any capacity of
knowing and serving God, which was not restored
to them also as a race in the gift of Jesus Christ,
then the proverb that "The fathers have eaten sour
grapes, and the children's teeth are set on edge,"
would have been true; but God, in asserting the
equality of His ways, denies the truth of this proverb in terms which mark that its truth would,
according to His judgment, be incompatible with
equality. I may here observe that this proverb is
amongst us also, and that its form now is,
"Although man by the fall has lost the power to obey,
God has not lost the right to demand obedience";
but, in any form, such a proverb God disclaims
as inconsistent with the equality of His ways.

The passage in Isaiah is equally clear in all these
points. "Now will I sing to my well-beloved a
song of my beloved touching His vineyard. My
beloved hath a vineyard in a very fruitful hill: and

He fenced it, and gathered out the stones thereof, and planted it with the choicest vine, and built a tower in the midst of it, and also made a wine-press therein : and He looked that it should bring forth grapes, and it brought forth wild grapes. And now, O inhabitants of Jerusalem, and men of Judah, judge, I pray you, between me and my vineyard. What could have been done more to my vineyard, that I have not done in it? wherefore, when I looked that it should bring forth grapes, brought it forth wild grapes?" (Isa. v. 1—4).

Here again it appeared to me that God's righteousness is assumed to be such as can be judged of and appreciated by man, even in his unregenerate state; for the invitation to judge is here addressed to the men of Judah and inhabitants of Jerusalem, the very criminals on whom the sentence is pronounced. It is before them that God pleads His cause, and what is the amount of His pleading? *The sufficiency of the provision made* for enabling them to meet His demand is that which He sets forth as the proof of His righteousness, both in making these demands and in punishing them for not meeting them. And this provision He lays before themselves, that they may say whether they can find any defect or inadequacy in it. He thus evidently assumes that the righteousness of His requirement and judgment is a righteousness of

17

which man can judge, and ought to judge, by the
same rule as that which he applies to his own conduct
and to that of his fellow-men. And He asserts that
His righteousness, when tried by this rule, will be
found conformable to it.

There are many passages in the Bible, both in
the Old and New Testaments, which are equally
strong and pointed with those which I have noticed,
against the generally received doctrine of election,
but I shall not at present cite more, as my reader
may probably be in the condition in which I was
myself when first these things were presented to
me. I acknowledged the force of the passages—I
acknowledged my inability to interpret them in
consistency with the doctrine of election—I fully
admitted the responsibility of man and the righteousness of God—but I could not allow any logical
conclusions of my own understanding to interfere
with my submission to the inspired word ; and therefore I still felt that whilst the 9th chapter of the
Epistle to the Romans continued to be an undisputed
part of Divine Revelation, it would be an act of
ungodly presumption in me to reject a doctrine
which appeared to be so manifestly contained in it.

I felt also that there was something in the
doctrine to which my own heart bore witness, as being
true to experience, as well as glorifying to God,
namely, that there was nothing good in man but

what was of the direct acting of the Spirit of God; and therefore I could not receive any argument against the doctrine which proceeded on the ground of an inherent self-quickening power in man.

What I required, then, in order really to free my conscience from the power of this doctrine, was to discover in the 9th chapter of the Epistle to the Romans, and some other similar passages, an unforced natural meaning, different from that which hitherto they had borne to me; and in that new meaning to find also what might correspond with my distinct experience of the action of the Spirit of God within me, in opposition to the spirit of my own will.

I continued then to read this dark chapter from time to time, hoping always that it would please God to give me further light upon it; for I felt quite free to do this in humility, because God had said, " Judge, I pray you, between me and my vineyard." The first ray of light that visited me in this course was in reading the 18th chapter of Jeremiah, to which the 21st verse of the 9th chapter of the Epistle to the Romans evidently refers. No part of the chapter appeared to me more dark than this 21st verse, for it seemed as if in it the apostle were claiming for God the right of making a man wicked and then denying to the man the right of complaining that he had been so made. " Nay but,

O man, who art thou that repliest against God?
Shall the thing formed say to him that formed
it, Why hast thou made me thus? Hath not the
potter power over the clay, of the same lump
to make one vessel unto honour, and another unto
dishonour?"

These verses do certainly seem to assert in unequivocal terms the Calvinistic doctrine of election;
but let us turn to the 18th chapter of Jeremiah, to
which they refer. In the beginning of that chapter
it is thus written: "The word which came to Jeremiah from the Lord, saying, Arise, and go down to
the potter's house, and there I will cause thee to
hear My words. Then I went down to the potter's
house, and, behold, he wrought a work on the wheels.
And the vessel that he made of clay was marred in
the hand of the potter: so he made it another vessel,
as seemed good to the potter to make it. Then the
word of the Lord came unto me, saying, O house of
Israel, cannot I do with you as this potter? saith
the Lord. Behold, as the clay is in the potter's
hand, so are ye in My hand, O house of Israel"
(vers. 1–6).

This passage, so far as we yet see, appears to
give full confirmation to the Calvinistic interpretation of the 9th chapter of the Romans. It seems
to say that as the potter has the right of making or
marring a vessel, as may appear good to him, so God

claims to Himself the right of making or marring
the character and condition of a man as seems good
to Him; and that as the potter in this particular
instance appeared to have chosen to mar a vessel,
so God would choose to mar the condition of some
men, without giving any reason but His own sovereign pleasure. Such a claim on the part of God
were indeed a fearful thing; but if this be really
the meaning of the passage, there is no replying to
it, and we must either acknowledge the Calvinistic
doctrine of election in its darkest extent, or deny
the authority of the Scriptures.

But this *is not* the true meaning of the passage,
as we shall see by merely going on to the following
verses, in which God Himself makes the application
of the spectacle which He had brought the prophet
to witness in the potter's house. " O house of
Israel, cannot I do with you as this potter ? saith
the Lord. Behold, as the clay is in the potter's
hand, so are ye in Mine hand, O house of Israel.
At what instant I shall speak concerning a nation,
and concerning a people, to pluck up, and to pull
down, and to destroy it ; *if that nation*, against whom
I have pronounced, *turn from their evil*, I will repent
of the evil that I thought to do unto them. And
at what instant I shall speak concerning a nation,
and concerning a kingdom, to build and to plant it ;
if it do evil in My sight, that it obey not My voice,

then I will repent of the good, wherewith I said I would benefit them. Now *therefore* go to, speak to the men of Judah, and to the inhabitants of Jerusalem, saying, Thus saith the Lord, *Behold, I frame evil against you, and devise a device against you*: RETURN YE NOW EVERY ONE *from his evil ways, and make his ways and his doings good*" (vers. 6–11).

I saw from this inspired application and interpretation of the action which the prophet witnessed in the potter's house, that what, to a superficial reader, appears to be the meaning of the passage, is not its real meaning. I saw that it contained a meaning not only different from, but opposed to the ordinary doctrine of election, for it declared that the future prospects of men were placed by God in their own hands; and that as God's promises and threatenings were addressed, not to individuals, but to characters, a man by changing his character might change God's dealing towards him. I saw that it was adduced for the purpose of maintaining, not that the potter had a right to make a vessel good or bad according to his own pleasure, but that he had a right, if a vessel turned out ill in his hands, to reject that vessel, and break it down, and make it up anew into another vessel. The right of making a thing bad is not contemplated at all in the passage—the matter considered is, whether the potter, after having once made a vessel, is bound to preserve it although it turns out quite unfit for the purpose for which it was made, or whether, in such a case, he has the right of rejecting it. And as the exercise of this right of rejection on the part of the potter is unquestioned, *although his works do not go wrong by their own fault*, much more does God claim to Himself the right of rejecting a people, whom He had set up for a particular purpose, *if they refused to answer that purpose.*

The decree of reprobation is not a decree which shuts in a man to sin and to punishment,—it is a decree which pronounces a sentence of punishment against sin; for thus it spoke to Adam, " *Because* thou hast hearkened to the voice of thy wife, and hast eaten of the tree," etc. And the decree of election does not shut in a man to holiness and blessedness, but pronounces a blessing on holiness; for thus it spoke to Christ, " Thou lovest righteousness, and hatest wickedness, *therefore* God, Thy God, hath anointed Thee with the oil of gladness above Thy fellows " (Ps. xlv. 7). The importance of this observation lies in this, that as Adam and Christ are the heads of the reprobation and the election, so they are also specimens of the way in which every individual falls under one or other of these sentences. They who follow the reprobate head, they are reprobate; they who follow the elect Head, they are elect.

But some one will say, this is true, but we must go farther back, to see what is the cause of this difference amongst men. What makes one man follow the reprobate head, and another the elect Head? We may seek to go farther back, but God does not go farther back; He has provided man with ability, and He lays the use of that ability to man's own door. Thus in accounting for a wicked man's turning away from his wickedness, He merely says, "*Because he considereth*, and turneth away from all his transgressions, he shall surely live" (Ezek. xviii. 29). And in like manner, in accounting for a wicked man continuing in his wickedness, He merely says, "Because I have called, *and ye refused*; I have stretched out My hand, *and no man regarded*," etc. (Prov. i. 24).

The difficulty that men feel in this matter is nothing else than the difficulty which they have in believing that God really has made a responsible creature with the power of choice between flesh and spirit, to whom He can truly and reasonably say, "I have set before thee, this day, life and death, blessing and cursing, therefore choose life."

The distinction between the election of sovereignty and the definitive election of judgment is plainly marked. God in sovereignty appoints the

conditions of His rational creatures, giving them
their provision of natural and spiritual gifts according to the place in the world or the Church which He
elects them to fill—He gives spiritual manifestations to one man, which He does not give to another;
in the same way as He gives greater intellectual
talents, or moral firmness, to one than to another.
But this is not the definitive election—it is only
an initiatory or provisional election. The definitive
election is the judicial election, which rests only on
those who rightly use their provision, whatever that
provision may be.

There is as great a diversity in the inward visitations of the Spirit sent to different persons as in
the outward events of their lives. Some are
visited by a sense of the presence of God and
of His love, producing, perhaps, a very joyful feeling in their souls; and some know little of such
visitations. Those who are favoured with them
are often tempted to think that religion consists
in having such things, and they therefore look out
for them, and seem to neglect the common course
of their lives which is unmarked by these lights, as
if it were shut out from religion, and even seem to
rest their hope before God on the fact of their
having had such manifestations. Whereas religion
does not consist in having such things at all, but
in the heart giving up its own will, and yielding

itself up to the will of God, known and felt in the conscience.

I do not mean to undervalue such manifestations of the Spirit any more than I have meant to undervalue the revelation of the outward word in the Bible ; all that I mean to say is, that both the one and the other are only *spiritual provision*, which may be bestowed without salvation, and may be withheld without perdition. If the steward of the five talents had hid them in the earth, he would, at the judgment, have been deprived of them, and been cast out as reprobate ; and if the steward of the one talent had been diligent in his little, he would have been judged faithful, and therefore he would have been chosen. "The Lord's delight is in them that fear Him, in them that hope in His mercy." He gives the gifts, but He asks the heart ; and on the answer of the heart His final judicial election is suspended. By His sovereign election He appoints to each man his provision; by His judicial election He rewards the faithful use of the provision. With the sovereign election man's will has nothing to do ; with the judicial election man's will has everything to do.

Out of the confounding of these two elections I believe has arisen, in a great measure, the common doctrine of election ; and that which has led to the confounding of them has been an inattention to, or a denial of, the fact that there is an inward spiritual provision bestowed even on those who neglect and misuse it—according to the warning in Ps. xxxii., " Be ye not like to horse and mule," following that word, " I will instruct thee and teach thee," etc.

We see two powers in every man—the one, the power of this world and of its prince ; and the other, the power of the world to come and of its Prince. These are the flesh and the Spirit, the seeds or principles of the first and second vessels. The man is not either the flesh or the Spirit, he is separate from both, but they are seeds sown in him, and his capacity of acting is merely his capacity of choosing to which of these two active principles he will yield himself up. They are, as it were, two cords attached to every heart, the one held by the hand of Satan, the other held by the hand of God. And they are continually drawing the heart in opposite directions, the one towards the things of self, the other towards the things of God—the one being the reprobation, and the other the election. Thus man in all his actings *never has to originate anything*; he has only to follow something already commenced within him; he has only to choose to which of these two powers he will join himself. Here, then, I found that which I had approved in Calvinism, and which I required

as an element of every explanation of the doctrine
which should be set up in opposition to Calvinism,
namely, a recognition that there is no self-quickening power in man, and that there is no good in
man but what is of the direct acting of the Spirit
of God.

I believe that it is the fear of attributing glory
to man in his own salvation, and of taking glory
from God, that attaches many people to the doctrines of Calvinism; but they would do well to
consider whether they are not, in fact, withholding
from God the glory which He desires in man, and
seeking to force upon Him a kind of glory which He
does not desire. God receives a glory to His *power*
in all the other works of His hands in this world,
but they give Him no glory which they can keep
back from Him. When He made man He made a
creature that might give Him a higher glory—a
glory *to His love*, a freewill offering, a glory which
it could keep back, but would not, because it loved
Him.

Is it to give glory to man, to say that once he
followed his own wisdom and leant on his own
strength, and that *then* he was always wrong and
always wretched, but that he has at last learned to
know the folly of his own wisdom, and the weakness of his own strength, and has believed God's
assurance that He is the true guide and portion of

man, and so has been persuaded to give up all confidence in himself or any creature, and to commit
himself to the Lord, and that *now* he knows righteousness and peace ?   I ask, is this to give glory
to man ?   Or, is it not rather a true description of
the glory which God desires from man ?

THE HEART MAKES THE THEOLOGIAN

A POOR, ignorant, naked savage, who knows and feels so much as this, that he is a sinner, that God hates sin and yet has mercy on the sinner, knows and believes more of the gospel than the most acute and most orthodox theologian, whose heart has never been touched by the love of God. The purest heart has the most correct faith, because it is susceptible of the truest impressions from holy love. It knows best what holy love means, and therefore it can believe best. Clear views of the gospel do not consist in having our logical lines all drawn accurately from premises to conclusion, but in having distinct and vivid impressions of the moral facts of the gospel, in all their meaning and all their importance.

There is an aphorism quoted by that holy and heavenly-minded man, Archbishop Leighton, but from what author I do not recollect, which, under the form of paradox, contains most sober and valuable counsel: "If you would have much faith, love much; and if you would have much love, believe much." We cannot love unless we discern amiableness, and this we can only do by the light of love. There is no puzzle in this. Every day we see cases analogous to it in common life. A man whose stomach has been ruined by artificial and highly exciting food, has no appetite for plain wholesome nourishment, and yet the only way to recover his appetite is to take this plain nourishment. This food has a natural suitableness to his appetite, and his appetite has a natural desire after such food, although that desire, from habitual misdirection, feels little excitement from it. As he takes the food, however, his appetite gets better, and as his appetite gets better he takes more food. Thus the food and the appetite act and react upon each other till the man's health is restored. Even so a diseased soul has no appetite for the truths of the gospel, and yet nothing but that truth can restore it to health. As the soul improves in health its desire after its proper food increases; that medicinal food gives additional health to the spiritual system, and this additional health is accompanied by an increase of desire after the truth.

Clear views of the character of God can exist only in minds whose affections are pure and strong and properly directed; and in perfect consistency with this, and as deeply rooted in the necessity of things, is the fact that the affections can only be purified and strengthened, and rightly directed, by being brought in contact with clear views of the character of God.   Thus perfect faith supposes perfect sanctification, and perfect sanctification supposes perfect faith.   What else is the meaning of a holy mind, than that it delights in and feeds on holy things ?   They are wrong who suppose that the sanctification of a soul consists simply in the truth's abiding in it; and they also are wrong who suppose that a soul can be sanctified by any other means.   An unholy soul has little susceptibility of impressions from holy objects ; and although they have a natural suitableness to its affections, yet it is scarcely moved or stirred when in contact with them, and when absent from them feels no desire after them.   Whereas a holy soul, in their absence, longs after them, and in their presence is increasingly susceptible of impressions from them ; and is at the same time increasingly unsusceptible of impressions from their opposites.

A GOSPEL FOR THE LIVING

WE have a simple scriptural test by which we may try all the views and interpretations of Christian doctrine: are they good and profitable in their influence on the heart and conduct? If they have not this tendency, if the impressions naturally made by them are not of this description, we may be assured that we have mistaken the doctrine.

Thus, if the view which we take of the doctrine of election, or a particular providence, be such a one as leads us to be negligent in our callings, or to consider ourselves free from moral responsibility, we may be sure that this is a wrong view, because it cannot be good or profitable to the characters of men.

The doctrine of election is just another name for the doctrine of free grace. It teaches that all men are under deserved condemnation, and therefore can have no claim on God for pardon ; and that this and all other mercies are the gifts of His *own free bounty and choice.* It thus teaches us humility and gratitude, by impressing us with the conviction that

18

we are debtors to God's unmerited bounty, not only for the gift of Christ and the knowledge of it, but also for the influence of the Spirit, which inclines our hearts to accept it.

The doctrine of a particular providence teaches that the same God who gave His Son to save us orders every event in our lot. The belief of this will dispel worldly fears and anxieties, and inspire confidence, and impress with a continued sense of the Divine presence ; and, far from producing care-lessness or recklessness with regard to the duties and the circumstances of life, it will draw forth the most attentive and sensitive and humble vigilance ; for it discovers to us the finger of God in everything, small or great, sorrowful or joyful.

It is possible that the doctrine of the persever-ance of the saints should be so perverted by the corruption of human nature as to lead to indolent security and unwatchful habits. But this is not the doctrine as stated in the Bible. The true doctrine is, that as it was God who first opened the eyes of sinners to the glory of the truth, so their continuance in the truth requires and receives the same almighty support to maintain it. It is not in their title to heaven, as distinct from the path to heaven, that they are maintained and persevere. No ; they " are kept by the power of God, *through faith* unto salvation." This doctrine, then, really leads to humble dependence on God, as the only support of our weakness; and to vigilance, from the knowledge that when we are not actually living by faith, we are out of that way in which believers are kept by the power of God unto salvation. The reality of our faith is proved only by our perseverance; if we do not persevere, we are not saints.

Any one of the doctrines of the atonement which can make us fearless or careless of sinning must be a wrong view, because it is not good nor profitable to men. That blessed doctrine declares sin pardoned, not because it is overlooked or winked at, but because the weight of its condemnation has been sustained on our behalf by our elder Brother and Representative. This makes sin hateful, by connecting it with the blood of our best Friend.

A GOSPEL FOR THE DYING

I can conceive nothing in this world more melancholy than the situation of a man, lying on his deathbed, who has before his mind all the rich treasures of the gospel, but does not see how he is to connect himself with them. He sees in the Bible the promises of God's everlasting love, and of the gift of eternal life, but he does not see them as his own, and he asks what and where is the link which unites a sinner to these unutterable blessings? Oh, it is an inquiry full of agony when death is evidently not many hours distant! If he is told that faith is the link which unites the sinner to the promises, he looks into himself to see whether his faith is right, and he cannot tell whether it is or is not, and his perplexity rises above his strength or his endurance, and his agitation makes it impossible for him to know or examine what the state of his belief is. Would it not be a blessed message to that soul to tell him that Christ died, not for believers, but for the world, that He was promised as a deliverer before there was one penitent or

believing thought in any human breast, and that
when He did appear on earth He said of Himself
that He came " to seek and to save that which was
lost," and His invitation was, " Come unto Me, all
ye that are weary and heavy laden, and I will give
you rest." God revealed those joyful truths to men,
not that they might be rewarded for believing them,
but that they might have much peace in resting on
them, and that their hearts might be filled with
much love and gratitude in thinking of and feeding
on the kindness of that God who has had mercy on
them.

Would it not be good tidings of great joy to
him to tell him that Christ had been given as a
propitiation for the sins of the whole world; and
" that in Him God was reconciling the world unto
Himself, not imputing unto them their trespasses ";
that thus the full pardon was already given to him
before he had thought of asking it; and that what
now remained for him was to bless God for His
unspeakable gift, and to ask for that spirit which
might open his understanding and his affections to
appreciate and to feel the value and the love of the
gift? When the poor man believed this, he would
be justified by faith, he would have the sense of
pardon and acceptance before God, and he would
speak to Him as to a father who pitieth his own
children. Before he believed this he was one of

that world which God so loved as to give His Son to be a propitiation for its sins; but whilst he remained ignorant of that love, and unbelieving, he was not justified by it, his conscience remained unpurged, he neither knew his sin nor his pardon, he had no childlike confidence in God, he had no share in eternal life.

A GOSPEL FOR THE NATURAL MAN

THE holy love of God is the attribute most glorified in the atonement. This is the crown; this gives its character to the whole work. The more polluted and depraved, therefore, a mind is, the less capable is it of understanding and believing the gospel.

And yet the gospel was sent into the world that the polluted and depraved might be saved by the faith of it, both from the condemnation and the power of sin. And well is it fitted for their case. Even in the most polluted and the most depraved there are feelings still remaining which, in the hour of sorrow or fear, may melt to the voice of kindness and compassion. There are in the storehouse of Providence events which will bring the stoutest heart to a stand, and force it to feel its weakness, and then the charge of guilt may refuse any longer to be despised, and the gracious invitations of an Almighty Father may not be disregarded.

The gospel is sent to our whole race, and therefore it is addressed to every variety of character. Every man has some accessible point in his heart, and to every such point is there a special message sent from heaven in the gospel. The moral faculties are no doubt diseased to a great degree, but though diseased they are not eradicated, and though generally directed to objects beneath them, and hurtful to them, they are not entirely dead to their true objects. There are great differences amongst men in this respect, as well from original constitution as from habit. Some spirits are so finely strung that they seem instinctively to vibrate to every high and generous tone, whilst others seem utterly destitute of any such sensations. In some the conscience has suffered the greatest degradation, and in others the affections. All are turned from God, but they are turned in different degrees and in different ways. Now the gospel is just suited to this diversity. And as in external nature, if the sense of smell is gone, the rose may still be presented to the eye, and if that also is gone, its structure and form may be learned by the touch, so in the spiritual system, if the imposing voice of holiness, bringing the charge of guilt against the sinner, fails to awaken his sleeping conscience, his understanding may still be accessible to the reasonableness of the system, or his affections to its kindness. I do not mean to say that one of these impressions will supply the want of the others—that an impression of the reasonableness of Christianity will fill

the place of an impression of its love or its holiness, but simply that it may prepare the way for
them by bringing the whole subject into near consideration.   The great matter is, that the mind,
with all its faculties, should come within the touch
and excitement of the gospel, and it is of small
importance where its influence commences, or in
what order it advances.   We have seen that it
addresses the higher faculties, but it often happens
that these are so blunted and obstinately misdirected, that they scarcely stir to the warning or
inviting voice.   It is therefore well becoming the
wisdom and the compassion of God to fit the
address also to other principles which are less
liable to disease or decay.   He has accordingly
directed it to the very elements of our nature—to
that instinct which, though misdirected, continues
always strong and sensitive.   I mean the principle
of self-preservation and the desire of happiness.

   This principle is a most powerful one.   Joy and
sorrow are mere expressions of self-love, and these
are our ruling feelings, and maintain their sway
most universally and constantly.   They are intimately connected with the sources of our love and
hatred, our hope and fear.   We love and hope
for that in which we find joy ; we dislike and
avoid and fear that in which we find sorrow.
These feelings exist and are in exercise in every

mind; and the character depends on the objects by which they are excited.

The form in which the gospel was announced by the angel to the shepherds of Bethlehem marks its distinguishing characteristic to be joy, and points to these natural instincts as the feelings to which it is addressed. "Behold," said the heavenly messenger,. "I bring you good tidings of great joy, which shall be to all people; for unto you is born this day, in the city of David, a Saviour, who is Christ the Lord." That promised seed had appeared who was destined to roll back the dark tide of human things, to bruise the serpent's head, and to break that reign of sin and sorrow and death under which the whole creation had so long groaned —He had come who was to retrieve a hundredfold the loss of that first paradise, bringing good out of evil, and life out of death, and who was to lay the foundations of a kingdom which shall never be removed, but shall grow and expand through unending ages. The promise was most general, it was given when sin and sorrow were first known on earth, and it was held forth as a remedy for both. And now the fulfilment had commenced. It was indeed a message of great joy. There may be, and assuredly are, many dark souls that could see no triumph in a deliverance from sin, but where is that being of our blood who could refrain from joy at the prospect of seeing sorrow and pain and death abolished for ever? This message then, although it speaks high things to a spiritual intelligence, addresses also the natural feelings.

Behold these feelings, and then contemplate the glorious character of God; and let us join in praise to Him who hath condescended, through such obscure avenues, to introduce the light of that character into the soul of man. If the gospel addressed merely our generous feelings, our love of what is right and excellent, our sense of what is beautiful and lovely, it would be a very different thing from what it is; it would be suited to another order of beings, and, with regard to us, would scarcely be deserving the name of glad tidings. But, blessed be the name of our God, He hath addressed us in that character which cleaves closest to us; He hath spoken to us as base and polluted, but, above all, as selfish beings. He meets the natural cry of misery, and the weary and undefined cravings of the unsatisfied spirit. His loudest and most general invitations, both in the Old and New Testaments, are addressed, not to the moral, but to the natural feelings; to the sense of misery, and the desire of happiness. " Ho, every one that thirsteth, come ye to the waters" (Isa. lv. 1). " Come unto Me, all ye that are weary and heavy laden, and I will give you rest" (Matt. xi. 28). " Who-

soever will, let him take of the water of life freely"
(Rev. xxii. 17). At this despised door of nature
the Saviour knocks, and through it He deigns to
enter. He came to bind up the broken heart, and
to comfort all that mourn. And many come, as it
seems, led by the mere instinctive longing after
enjoyment, and try the gospel as a last and forlorn
experiment, after the failure of every other attempt
to obtain happiness. And, oh, what an unlooked-
for discovery do they make! He who had found
no resting-place in the world, and who had wandered through it in quest of some object, however
insignificant, that might interest him, and for a
moment at least remove the sense of that hopeless
languor which lay dead upon his heart, finds now
an object which his widest desires cannot grasp,
even filial communion with God here, and the full
enjoyment of Him through a magnificent eternity,
on the very threshold of which he already stands.
He who has felt himself too weak to resist the
storms and roughnesses of life learns to lean with
confidence on Omnipotence. He whose conscience
of sin has made life a burden to him, and at the
same time has taught him to look with a vague
horror to futurity, applies to that fountain which
was opened in the house of David for sin and for
uncleanness, and he has peace with God, through
faith in Jesus Christ.

EVIL

THE permission of evil is the great mystery. Is it not a mystery that God should be *omnipotent love*, and yet that the world should be just a vast cauldron boiling over with violence and pollution and misery? It is no wonderful thing that a world of sin should be a world of sorrow; this requires no explanation. The creature away from God is necessarily away from blessedness, and it is right that it should be so. But the existence, the permitted and prolonged existence of a sinning and sorrowing world, is a riddle; and the triumph of darkness over light is a riddle; and the affliction of God's children is a riddle. *Can* God not help this, or *will* He not? We are living and moving and having our being in the midst of this mighty riddle—it meets us everywhere—it encloses us as a net on every hand, and man's wisdom can find no outlet, no solution. And amongst the many marvels that are to be found in man's character and condition, there are few greater than

this, that he should be able to contemplate himself
and his condition without astonishment, and as if
there were nothing in them to be wondered at.
It is indeed a mighty riddle. It is God's riddle,
and none can solve it but God. God's word contains the solution of it. This is the *secret of the
Lord*, which is with them that fear **Him**; and it
consists in the knowledge of God and of Jesus
Christ whom He hath sent.

Man charges God with the existence of evil,
and exculpates himself. God declares that evil
has arisen from the creature's seeking to be independent of God, and so shutting God out from it.
God is not the author of evil. He is good, and He
abhorreth evil, and desireth its destruction. The
death of Christ is the expression of God's abhorrence to evil, of God's incompatibility with evil.
If God were the author of evil, there would be no
hope for man. But although God is not the
author of evil, although He created all things very
good, yet He has permitted evil to enter and mar
the good. Now, why is this? A good rising out
of evil is the solution of the mystery,—a higher,
a nobler, and more blessed good than that which
the evil had destroyed, and a good which could be
produced only by the destruction of evil. The
whole Bible is just a varied unfolding of this
mystery—a varied revelation of this purpose, in

order that man, by the knowledge of it, might be
carried forward through and beyond the present
evil to embrace a future good which is to arise
out of it.   This hope is the anchor of the soul—it
is the hope by which we are saved.

PRAYER

It appears to me further, that the invitation to prayer is itself an act of forgiveness. And the invitation to prayer is universal; whoever will make use of it may make use of it. There is no limit but in the will of man. The proof of this contained in the denunciation of Peter on Simon (Acts viii. 20–24) is very strong. He tells him that he is in the gall of bitterness and bond of iniquity, and yet he desires him to pray. And never has there been a prayer lost. Some of my readers may recollect an anecdote told of Buonaparte, which in some degree illustrates my meaning. When the Duc d'Enghien was apprehended, it is said that he begged much for a personal interview with Buonaparte. This, however, Buonaparte decidedly refused; and being afterwards asked his reason for doing so, he replied, "I should have been obliged to pardon him if I had admitted him, and I had resolved that he should die." Hear what this unjust judge saith,—he would have considered the reluctantly

granted admission of his victim into his presence
as inferring a pardon, — surely then he would
have considered his own pressing invitation to
him to come into his presence as still more
strongly inferring a pardon. If that hard
man felt thus, what shall we conclude from
the invitations which the God of love makes to
all? What shall we conclude from the invitations
of Him, who willeth not the death of the sinner,
but that all should turn and live? of Him who
said, "Come unto Me, all ye that are weary and
heavy laden, and I will give you rest"? It may
be said that it is only the prayer of faith which
is heard. This is true; but every prayer to God
is a prayer of faith. It is not, and cannot be, a
prayer at all, without the belief that "God is,
and that He is the rewarder of them that dili-
gently seek Him." We may pray for faith; we
may pray for the spirit of prayer; we may pray
for the waiting eye, and the hungering and thirst-
ing after righteousness; we may pray for the first
elements of Christian light and feeling, just as
well as for the communications of heavenly joy
and the greatest advancements in the Divine life.
But the first breathing or cry of the heart after
these things implies faith in God. And such
prayers, if real, are prayers in the name of Christ,
because they are prayers for the accomplishment of

19

that work which Christ came from heaven to do.
The name of God is not the word *God*, but the
revealed character of God; and the name of Christ
is the character of God revealed in Christ,—the
character of holy love,—consuming sin and saving
the sinner. He came to destroy the works of the
devil,—this is His name,—and a prayer against the
works of the devil is a prayer in His name, being
according to the will and counsel of God revealed
in Him. This seems to be the meaning of that
frequently recurring expression, "in the name of
Christ." When the heart goes along with the
declared purpose of God, to eradicate evil and
bring in the reign of righteousness,—it prays in
the name of Christ,—it lives and moves and has
its being in the name of Christ. Prayer seems
to suppose an open ear and a forgiving heart; and
when God commands it, He seems to manifest
Himself as the hearer of prayer and the forgiver
of sins.

VAIN RELIGION

MEN are apt to think that religion is just one of the many duties of life, and that it ought to have its own time and its own place like the others,—and they set apart for it churches and Sundays and certain other occasions,—and having done so much for it, they seem to consider it an intruder if it appears out of these limits. Thus we know that although the authority of God and the inspiration of the Bible are nominally acknowledged in this country, yet any one who, in the great deliberative assemblies of the nation, for instance, should quote the Bible as a reason for giving his vote one way or another would be generally regarded either as a fanatic or a canter. The introduction of such a book, or such an authority, would be considered almost as great an impropriety as the introduction of a band of music. Now, religion is not just one of the many duties of life; it is itself a life; it is the taking a man off from his own root and grafting him on God as the new root of all his thoughts and desires and doings. And as the sap of the root circulates through every branch and twig and leaf of the tree, so the love of God, which is the sap of this new spiritual root, ought to circulate through every thought and desire and action of the man. If a man were truly religious, he would judge of everything by the light of God's will; and this will of God would be given as the reason of his judgment whenever he was asked for his reason. And amongst those who, *not nominally, but really* acknowledged the authority of God, such a reason would be considered as the only good reason which could be given. God is not really acknowledged in any country where His authority cannot be appealed to as a ground of judgment or of action without exciting astonishment. I mention this as a striking feature in the public character of the nation. The same men who would scout the mention of the Bible in one place would have no objections to it in another; they go to church, and even to Bible and Missionary Societies perhaps. All that they insist on is, that religion should keep its own place. They know it only as a decency; they do not know it as *the great truth,*—the paramount relation of their being,—as that which, according as it is present or absent, determines the character of every thought, word, or action, to be either right or wrong essentially.

A philosophical critic would have had much delight in remarking the skill with which Demosthenes selected his topics and arguments so as to excite those feelings in his audience which were favourable to his own cause; but this philosophical delight left his passions unmoved and his conduct uninfluenced. It was the orator's wish to gain his cause, and this he could only do by moving the affections and convincing the judgment of the Athenians. But the affections could not be moved, nor the judgment convinced, unless his statements and arguments were received as substantial truth in themselves, altogether independent of philosophical relation and harmony. Had he delivered a critical analysis of his famous oration for the crown, instead of the oration itself, it is probable that he, and not Eschines, would have been exiled. It is proper that this beautiful relation should be seen and admired; but if it comes to be the prominent object of belief, the great truth of Christianity is not believed. A teacher of religion who should fill his discourses with the delineation of this relation might be a very entertaining and interesting preacher, but it is probable that he would not make many converts to Christianity. Our affections are excited by having corresponding objects presented to them, not by observing that there does exist such a relation between the affections and their objects. A man under the sentence of death may well and naturally rejoice when he hears that he is pardoned; but it will be no consolation to him to be informed that there is a natural connexion between receiving a pardon in such circumstances and rejoicing. As the blood flowed no better through Harvey's veins than it does through the veins of many who never heard of the theory of circulation, so an acquaintance with the relation which subsists between moral impressions and their exciting causes does not give the philosopher any advantage, in point of moral susceptibility, over the peasant who never heard of such a relation.

There is a belief in Christianity as a subject of controversy which deserves a severer censure than merely that it is incapable of doing any moral good. The great facts of revelation are not the object of which this belief is the impression. The real object of faith in a believer of this order is, that his view is right and that of his opponent wrong. The impression from this object is naturally approbation of himself and contempt of others.

A man who forms a judgment upon any subject on reasonable grounds cannot but believe that an opposite judgment is wrong; if he does not believe this, he has formed no judgment on the matter. But this ought not to be the prominent object of belief. If it be, the character is ruined. There is not in the world a more hateful thing than to see the gospel of Jesus Christ converted into a piece of ambitious scholarship or of angry contention; an angel of light and peace transformed into the demon of pride, of darkness and discord. But the person who falls into this sinful calamity does not believe the gospel; he believes in his own superiority and intelligence, and in another's inferiority and ignorance. These are his objects, and fatal must their impression be. The object presented to our faith in the gospel is the character of God manifested in Jesus Christ as the just God and yet the Saviour. It is the remission of sins through the blood of atonement shed for us by love unutterable. It is God in our nature standing on our behalf as our elder brother and representative, bearing the punishment which we had deserved, satisfying the law which we had broken, and, on the ground of this finished work, proclaiming sin forgiven, and inviting the chief and the most wretched of sinners to become a happy child of God for ever and ever. This object is presented to our belief, not as a theme of polemical discussion, but that it may stamp on our souls its own image, the likeness of God.

HAPPINESS

WHEN it is said that happiness is necessarily and exclusively connected with a resemblance to the Divine character, it is evident that the word "happiness" must be understood in a restricted sense. It cannot be denied that many vicious men enjoy much gratification through life ; nor can it even be denied that this gratification is derived in a great measure from their very vices. This fact is, no doubt, very perplexing, as every question must be which is connected with the origin of evil. But still, it is no more perplexing than the origin of evil, or than the hypothesis that our present life is a state of trial and discipline. Temptation to evil evidently implies a sense of gratification proceeding from evil ; and evil could not have existed without this sense of gratification connected with it. So, also, this life could not be a state of trial and discipline in good unless there were some inducement or temptation to evil—that is, unless there were some sense of gratification attending evil. It probably does not lie within the compass of human faculties to give a completely satisfactory answer to these questions ; whilst yet it may be rationally maintained that if there is a propriety in this life being a state of discipline, there must also be a propriety in sin being connected with a sense of gratification. But then, may not this vicious gratification be extended through eternity, as well as through a year or an hour ? I cannot see any direct impossibility in this supposition on natural principles ; and yet I feel that the assertion of it sounds very much like the contradiction of an intuitive truth.

There is a great difference between the happiness enjoyed with the approbation of conscience and that which is felt without it or against it. When the conscience is very sensitive, the gratification arising from vice cannot be very great. The natural process, therefore, by which such gratifica-tion is obtained or heightened is by lulling or deadening the conscience. This is accomplished by habitually turning the attention from the distinction of good and evil, and directing it to the circum-stances which constitute vicious gratification.

The testimony of conscience is that verdict which every man returns for or against himself upon the question, whether his moral character has kept pace with his moral judgment ? This verdict will therefore be, in relation to absolute moral truth, correct or incorrect, in proportion to the degree of illumination possessed by the moral judgment; and the feeling of remorse will be more or less painful according to the inequality which subsists between the judgment and the character. When a man, therefore, by dint of perseverance, has brought this judgment down to the level of his character, and has trained his reason to call evil good and good evil, he has gained a victory over conscience and expelled remorse. If he could maintain this advantage through his whole existence, his conduct would admit of a most rational justification. But then, his peace is built solely on the darkness of his moral judgment; and therefore all that is necessary in order to make him miserable, and to stir up a civil war within his breast, would be to throw such a strong and undubious light on the perfect character of goodness as might extort from him an acknowledgment of its excellency, and force him to contrast with it his own past history and present condition. Whilst his mental eye is held in fascination by this glorious vision, he cannot but feel the anguish of remorse; he cannot but feel that he is at fearful strife with some mighty and mysterious being, whose power has compelled even his own heart to execute vengeance on him; nor can he hide from himself the loathsomeness and pollution of that spiritual pestilence which has

poisoned every organ of his moral constitution.
He can hope to escape from this wretchedness
only by withdrawing his gaze from the appalling
brightness ; and, in this world, such an attempt can
generally be made with success. But suppose him
to be placed in such circumstances that there
should be no retreat—no diversity of objects which
might divert or divide his attention—and that,
wherever he turned, he was met and fairly con-
fronted by this threatening Spirit of Goodness, it
is impossible that he could have any respite from
misery except in a respite from existence. If this
should be the state of things in the next world,
we may form some conception of the union there
between vice and misery.

Whilst we stand at a distance from a furnace, the
effect of the heat on our bodies gives us little
uneasiness ; but, as we approach it, the natural
opposition manifests itself, and the pain is increased
by every step that we advance. The complicated
system of this world's business and events forms, as
it were, a veil before our eyes, and interposes a kind
of moral distance between us and our God, through
which the radiance of His character shines but
indistinctly, so that we can withhold our attention
from it if we will. The opposition which exists
between His perfect holiness and our corrupt
propensities does not force itself upon us at every

step. His views and purposes may run contrary
to ours ; but as they do not often meet us in the
form of a direct and personal encounter, we contrive
to ward off the conviction that we are at hostility
with the Lord of the Universe, and think that we
may enjoy ourselves in the intervals of these much-
dreaded visitations, without feeling the necessity
of bringing our habits into a perfect conformity
with His. But when death removes this veil, by
dissolving our connexion with this world and its
works, we may be brought into a closer and more
perceptible contact with Him who is of purer eyes
than to behold iniquity. In that spiritual world
we may suppose that each event, even the minutest
part of the whole system of government, will bear
such an unequivocal stamp of the Divine character
that an intelligent being, of opposite views and
feelings, will at every moment feel itself galled and
thwarted and borne down by the direct and over-
whelming encounter of this all-pervading and
almighty mind. And here it should be remembered
that the Divine government does not, like human
authority, skim the surface, nor content itself with
an unresisting exterior and professions of submission, but comes close to the thoughts, and
carries its summons to the affections and the will,
and penetrates to those recesses of the soul where,
whilst we are in this world, we often take a pride

and a pleasure in fostering the unyielding sentiments of hatred and contempt, even towards that
superiority of force which has subdued and fettered
and silenced us.

The man who believes in revelation will, of
course, receive this view as the truth of God ; and
even the unbeliever in revelation, if he admits the
existence of an almighty Being of a perfect moral
character, and if he see no unlikelihood in the
supposition that the mixture of good and evil, and
the process of moral discipline connected with it,
are to cease with this stage of our being, even he
cannot but feel that there is a strong probability in
favour of such an anticipation.

We see, then, how vicious men may be happy to
a certain degree in this world, and yet be miserable
in the next, without supposing any very great
alteration in the general system of God's government, and without taking into account anything
like positive infliction as the cause of their misery.
And it may be observed that this view gives
to vice a form and an extent and a power very
different from what is generally ascribed to it
amongst men. We are here conversant chiefly
about externals, and therefore the name of vice is
more commonly applied to external conduct than to
internal character. But in the world of spirits it
is not so. *There*, a dissonance in principle and

object from the Father of Spirits constitutes vice, and is identified with unhappiness. So that a man who has here passed a useful and dignified life, upon principles different from those of the Divine character, must, when under the direct action of that character, feel a want of adjustment and an opposition which cannot but mar or exclude happiness. Thus, also, the effects of pride, of vanity, or of selfishness, when combined with prudence, may often be most beneficial in the world ; and yet, if these principles are in opposition to God's character, they must disqualify the minds in which they reign for participating in the joys of heaven. The joys of heaven are described in Scripture to consist in a resemblance to God, or in a cheerful and sympathising submission to His will ; and as man naturally follows the impulse of his own propensities, without reference to the will of God, it is evident that a radical change of principle is necessary in order to capacitate him for that happiness.

It was to produce this necessary and salutary change that the gospel was sent from heaven. It bears upon it the character of God. It is not therefore to be wondered at that those whose principles are opposed to that character should also be opposed to the gospel. Christianity thus anticipates the discoveries of death. It removes the

veil which hides God from our sight ; it brings the
system of the spiritual world to act upon our
consciences ; it presents us with a specimen of
God's higher and interior government ; it gives us
a nearer view of His character in its true pro-
portions, and thus marks out to us the points
in which we differ from Him ; it condemns with His
authority ; it smiles and invites with His uncompromising purity. The man who dislikes all this
will reject Christianity and replace the veil, and
endeavour to forget the awful secrets which it
conceals ; and may perhaps be only at last roused
from his delusion by finding himself face to face
before the God whose warnings he had neglected,
and whose offers of friendship he had disregarded—
offers which, had they been accepted, would have
brought his will into concord with that sovereign
will which rules the universe, and fitted him to take
a joyful and sympathising interest in every part of
the Divine administration.

HEAVEN

SOME moralists have thought that the hope of heaven taints the purity of virtue by destroying its disinterestedness. But they do not know what heaven is. It is the sense of his spiritual corruption, rather than the sense of sorrow, which makes the Christian long after heaven. The holiness of heaven is still more attractive to him than its happiness. In heaven also the affections meet, and are for ever united to their proper object. They are filled and satisfied with the presence of God. It is this that they thirst after. They desire His favourable presence as their chief good. It is an interest undoubtedly—the highest interest. But is it a selfish interest? Shall the desire of a son, to behold once more the face of his father, after a few years of absence, be esteemed a pure and generous desire; and shall the desire of a spirit, long exiled from its native sphere, to return to its Father and its God, the centre of its being, the fountain of light and life and love, be called a selfish or interested desire? No, it is a pure desire which is sent down into the spirit from the heart of God, and which remains unsatisfied until it has again mingled with its source. No, it is a noble desire, and speaks a noble origin. And the fear connected with the idea of missing this object is not a base fear—it is the horror which a pure spirit feels at the thought of mixing with pollution, and of being tainted by it. The desire of doing that which is right for its own sake is in truth a part of the Christian's desire after heaven.

When a man says, " I believe the gospel, and therefore I am warranted to expect pardon and eternal life," I cannot but have doubts whether he understands the gospel. For if he did understand it I do not think that he would look further than the gospel itself as the reward of his faith. Let me suppose the case of a mother, whose only child has been stolen from her in infancy, and whose heart still bears the fresh and unclosed wound of her loss, and whose imagination is continually haunted with dark and busy thoughts as to what the present condition and future fate of her child may be. I discover the child, and find it all that a mother could wish or love. I come to her, and say to her that I have news for her, and that she will be richly rewarded if she believes them. I then tell her my news. Oh, reader ! do you think that she would ask me what reward I meant to give her for believing ?

The good which we receive from believing in the love of God, manifested in Christ Jesus, is analogous to that which we receive from believing in the worth and kindness of a human friend—only that the one is as nothing in comparison with the other. It is nothing else than the enjoyment of God in Himself and in His creatures. It is not anything that we get on account of our loving Him, but it is the happiness of loving Him, and knowing ourselves to be loved by Him. It is dwelling on and in His high perfections. It is giving Him our perfect sympathy and receiving His. It is knowing Him as the infinite God, and yet as an affectionate Father, as a friend that sticketh closer than a brother. It is the assurance which the heart draws, from His love in giving His Son, and perhaps from some more special and personal tokens of that love, that He will never leave us nor forsake us, that He will never cease to love us with a love which will be, and must be, our satisfying and filling and delighting portion through all eternity. It is the joyful and confident anticipation of the day when the mystery of God shall be accomplished, and the glory of the Lord shall be revealed, and when the children of God shall be glad, and rejoice for ever in the new heavens and the new earth which their Father shall create. It is the discovering that all the works of creation—all events—

time and space—eternity and infinity—everything
is full of that God who loved us and gave Himself
for us; and who, in giving us Himself, freely gives
us all things. This is the good that a soul gets by
believing the gospel; and is it not enough, or shall we
still ask whether we are warranted to expect pardon
and eternal life because we believe the gospel? Does
not such question indicate a radical mistake as to
the meaning of the gospel? Is it not the question
of a man who sees nothing in the gospel itself to
satisfy him, and therefore supposes that there must
surely be something else to accompany it in order
to make it that desirable thing which it is said to
be? Is it not the question of a man who considers
his belief of the gospel nothing else than a meritorious submission of his reason to the authority of God
—a submission which is to be rewarded by some
mark of His approbation?

CONCLUSION

READER, farewell. I believe that what I have written is according to the word of God; and as far as it is so I may look up to Him for a blessing on it. It would be an unspeakable joy to me to have any reason to think that it has been really honoured by Him to be the bearer of a message to your soul. At all events, I trust it may not do you the injury of exciting the spirit of controversy in you. If you don't agree with it, lay it down and go to the Bible; and if you do agree with it, in like manner lay it down and go to the Bible, and go in the spirit of prayer to Him whose word the Bible is, and ask of Him, and He will lead you into all truth—He will give you living water.

THE END

INDEX

www.ingramcontent.com/pod-product-compliance
Lightning Source LLC
Chambersburg PA
CBHW060534030726
47498CB00004B/1187